MANHATTAN ROCK PARTY

SAVANNAH WYLDE

Manhattan Rock Party
By Savannah Wylde
Copyright © 1982, 2024
Cover art by Fotor
ISBN print: 978-91-89822-48-1
ISBN e-book: 978-91-89822-49-8
Published by Yabot AB, Sweden, 2024

1 – The College for Women

As dawn streaked across the skyline, sending slanting rays of light through the Venetian blinds in Jennifer Davis' college room, she tossed and turned fitfully, unable to sleep. Only two more days until graduation at Luna Meadows College for Women. The ivy-covered old brick walls had been home to Jennifer for four long years. She loved the campus. In springtime, it was wonderful. The green shade trees lined the sidewalks like friendly sentinels, offering their lavish spreading protection.

Jennifer loved the memories of her college days. The first three years had been such exciting fun. She had shared them with her roommate, Susan Moore. Now that Susan was gone, she felt empty and alone.

This morning, she felt particularly restless and desperate for something to happen. She wished that her mother or father could see her at graduation time. But her father was a busy corporate attorney in Los Angeles and couldn't leave his thriving practice. As for her mother, she was always too occupied with her social activities to pay much attention to Jennifer.

A strange feeling of uneasiness disturbed Jennifer this morning. Sometimes, she longed to change her whole appearance. If she looked different, she reasoned, wouldn't her life be different?

Jennifer Davis was a shapely young girl who always aroused

interested male glances. Her hair was a rich golden color, and she was never quite sure whether she was a bright blonde or a pale redhead. Her eyes were in doubt, too. Sometimes, they were green when she wore certain colors; other times, they were deep lagoon blue.

She tossed and turned in her bed and pulled the covers over her. It was still chilly, and she always slept in the nude.

Jennifer couldn't help feeling that the years were rolling by too quickly. Nothing seemed to be happening to her. Nothing important, at least. Yes, she would soon be receiving her college degree and searching for a bookkeeper job in the field in which she had majored. However, her life seemed to stretch out on an endless, gloomy road. She couldn't help but wonder what destiny would do to her future. Her father had said that he would help her find a place in Charlotte, North Carolina, but she really didn't want to live there.

She sighed, and her pretty young face was sullen for a moment. But just for a short moment, for Jennifer would never allow her spirits to stay down for long. She always bounced back like a rubber ball, no matter what happened or how grim things became. She knew something good had to happen, for she was an almost incurable optimist.

Finally, she heard the sound of the alarm clock announcing it was time for her to get up. Throwing the covers back swiftly, she got out of bed. Looking at herself in the mirror, she couldn't help wishing that her girlfriend was back with her again. Susan Moore had been so fond of her. They had enjoyed each other so much. As Jennifer looked at her naked reflection, she admired her supple, firm bosoms, which stood up proudly. Then, letting her hand wander down to her crotch, she imagined how stimulating and exciting it would be if, once more, Susan would let her tongue slide around her thighs.

Jennifer couldn't disguise the sexual desire that she had now. Returning to the bed for a moment, she suddenly let her fingers slip into her vagina. Rolling over, she watched herself in the sliding mirrored doors of the bedroom's closet. She could observe her fingers gently massaging her crotch.

Jennifer lay back luxuriantly and inserted her finger. Vividly, she recalled the first time the beautiful brunette girl had let her eyes roam over her naked curvaceous body. She remembered how she had protested when Susan came over to her, completely naked, and threw her arms around her. Susan had laughed it off.

"It's not a big deal, honey," she remembered Susan saying. "Lots of girls make it with both sexes. One doesn't spoil you for the other."

Yet Jennifer had thought it was terrible that first time. Eventually, almost powerless to restrain herself, she had given in to Susan's insistence that they engage in female lovemaking. She had stretched out and spread her thighs for the beautiful brunette. The next thing she knew, Susan Moore was burying her face in Jennifer's lush, satiny-soft breasts. Susan had gone to work eagerly with her hungry mouth. Catching her breath sharply as she recalled the intimate lesbian caresses, it sent chills racing through Jennifer's body now.

The voluptuous young woman arched her back and bit her lip to keep from crying out. She thrilled to the kissing and remembered all too well how Susan's moist pink tongue slipped over the velvety flesh surrounding her bosoms. Susan's soft hands had roamed over her sleek, naked body, caressing her hips and inner thighs and promising even more personal contact. Vividly, Jennifer recalled what her roommate had said that first time.

"Hmmmm, you've got such a beautiful body, baby," Susan had purred in an admiring tone as her lips nibbled on one taut nipple, while she spoke. "Such lovely breasts!" Susan had told her. "So full, so firm. I love to suck and lick on them."

Flattery had won her over and taken her off guard. Susan's smooth, soft-sell approach had stimulated her. She recalled the rough men who had tried to assault her in the past and how she had been repelled by their advances. But now, as her young girlfriend, naked and beautiful, played with her ripe, young bosoms, she found her body tingling with raw physical sensations that she never knew existed.

Jennifer's proud nipples had become taut with female erectness. She was instantly shocked and dismayed that a girl was loving her, for she had been told it was so shameful. Yet, as she experienced such euphoric sensations, the guilt was disappearing, and she wanted her to proceed.

Susan had told her to relax. She had told her she was too inhibited, and there was really nothing to it. The young college girl's bosoms responded to Susan's licking and sucking. But at the same time, her mind was telling her over and over that she was doing the wrong thing, torturing her with an ominous cloak of shame and degradation.

"Relax, relax," Susan had insisted.

At this point, the young girl's bosoms had been teased

into full sexual anticipation. Susan began moving her head downward over the wide expanse of incredibly smooth feminine flesh. At the same instant, her hand stroked along her inner thighs and gradually began fondling and stroking her voluptuous, throbbing young pussy. The entire area was damp and sticky, and the intimate contact with another female's fingers made the beautiful young girl squirm with sensuous movements.

Closing her eyes now and recapturing this erotic instant vividly, Jennifer plunged her fingers into her own liquid vagina. She recalled, as shivers of excitement tingled through her body, how much pleasure she had discovered when Susan panted, "You've got such a beautiful pussy, baby. I love it."

She whispered as her probing fingers lazily separated the outer folds of her cunt and caressed the wet interior. "Anyone would be lucky to eat your pussy," Susan told her. "It's so pink and soft and wet."

Even though Jennifer Davis had been embarrassed earlier, now she was thrilled by the expert feminine caresses of her female lover. Jennifer blushed hotly as she found herself aroused beyond belief, squirming like a kitten as she went on playing with her clitoris. Her vibrant young pussy was sopping wet and tingling with pleasant erotic sensations that radiated through the rest of her body. Biting her lip to control her feelings, she watched as Susan stretched out at a right angle to her body, preparing to press her brunette head into her wet thicket.

"Hhmmm, beautiful, baby," Susan had exclaimed as she

gazed fondly at the brightly pink feminine pussy from closer range.

Keeping the outer labia separated with her fingers, she pressed her face hotly against the palpitating pussy with her long red tongue extended. She was actually doing it! This excited Jennifer more as she stimulated herself with her own fingertips.

When it had happened the first time, Jennifer had gasped with dual feelings of horror and fascination as Susan's tongue introduced her to the forbidden pleasures of cunnilingus. A second twinge of conscience told her to stop, yet the urgent physical needs of her vibrant young body became paramount. Although for an instant she was stricken by guilt about the sexually perverse act that she was permitting, she had soon surrendered completely, throwing her legs over Susan's shoulders.

"Ohhh, yes, yes," she had gasped in a breathless voice. "It feels so good. I never felt anything like it."

Susan's face had been plastered against the succulent, pungently perfumed feminine nest. Her tongue moved up and down with quick, serpentine flicks. The experienced older girl knew exactly what she was doing as her busy tongue found every sensitive nerve ending in the young girl's pink furrow. It only took seconds before Jennifer's tiny clitoris was swollen almost to the bursting point as the lovely young girl found herself totally entranced in the snares of her lesbian lover's tongue.

"Ohhh, I love it," she exclaimed, her voice catching. "Don't stop. It feels so good. So good! So very... good... ooohhhh!"

Never once pulling her face from the hot, wet feminine temple, Susan maneuvered around until she was kneeling between her female lover's shapely thighs. Her hands smoothly slid under Jennifer's soft buttocks, elevating her slightly, making her pussy all the more accessible. Becoming more and more enthralled in total sensual abandonment by the lewd caresses, the young college girl had thrown her bare legs over her shoulders and allowed them to dangle down her back.

"How do you like it, honey?" Susan smiled, her lips nibbling at the outer lips of Jennifer's pussy as she spoke.

"I... I love it," Jennifer gasped in a joyous voice. "It feels so good. I never dreamed another girl could..."

Stimulated and pleased by the young woman's willing confession, Susan kissed her wet box up and down its full length, quickly going back to work with her tongue. Jennifer jumped as if given a jolt of electricity as the brunette girl's tongue sliced through her vulva folds and into the bubbling interior. Her thighs coiled reflexively around Susan's head, and she began thrusting her pelvis back and forth in quick, jerky thrusts.

"Ohhh," Jennifer cried out, "it feels so... ooohhh... ohhhh so good!"

At this point, Susan was swimming in the swirling rapids of Jennifer's delectable pussy. Susan began concentrating all of her efforts on the young girl's magic button. The lust-crazed membrane was twitching and rigid with feminine erectness. Susan began sucking it between her lips, simultaneously flicking it with her capable tongue. The expert assault shattered Jennifer's body like a bolt of lightning.

"Ohhh," she had gasped, "you're driving me crazy!"

With her eyes shut tight, Jennifer Davis could remember every vivid detail of Susan's wild lovemaking. Her entire body was jerking spasmodically now as she pumped her fingers in rhythmically. She remembered how she had clenched her fists, pounding them against the bed. The highly aroused young college girl was thrilled with the delicious torments of lesbian love. Her voluptuous young breasts felt rock hard, and her dripping pussy was as hot as an oven.

"Ahhh, ohhhh," she gasped, panting and breathing heavily.

Knowing that she was on the verge of completely conquering her voluptuous roommate, Susan Moore redoubled her efforts with her mouth and tongue. Jennifer's hotly swollen membrane sucked between her lips as she drank in the wet gushes of pussy juice with slurping loud sounds that could be distinctly heard over Jennifer's heavily labored breathing.

The young girl's thighs were locked like a vise around her brunette head, and Jennifer's frantic hands were clawing excitedly through her lover's hair to urge her on.

Just thinking of it now was carrying Jennifer closer, ever closer, to a juicy, sticky climax.

"Ohhh, ahhhh, I'm coming!" Jennifer had cried out ecstatically.

She was unable to endure the delicious torment another moment longer. Jennifer's body dissolved in orgasmic spasms of exquisite intensity and duration. Breathless now and nearly crying out with arousal, Jennifer could hardly believe the rapturous clitoral convulsions that left her body simply quaking.

At the same instant, Jennifer Davis felt herself coming. The ecstatic memories of her female lover could always do this for her. She pumped her pelvis forward as her fingers stabbed in her hot, juicing pussy.

"Yes, yes," she gasped as she felt herself responding to the delicious pleasures of juicing.

Slowly Jennifer eased her fingers from her hot vagina. How she wished that, at this instant, she could spread her thighs for her girlfriend to lick her there. Pulling her fingers from her vagina, she gazed excitedly at her hair-fringed fissure. Then she came back to reality, recognizing she would have to hurry, for she had a class in about half an hour.

It didn't take her long to slip out of bed and get in the shower. As the refreshing shower water reminded her of the day ahead, she wondered if anyone she knew would be there to see her graduate. It did seem terrible that she had worked so hard and so long to be unable to share this proud moment with anyone. At the very time when she would appreciate having someone there, she would have no one.

Stepping out of the shower, Jennifer once more looked at her naked reflection in the mirror. Yes, she was a shapely girl. Her stunning, lustrous golden hair fell about her shoulders. Jennifer's eyes sparkled with delight as she thought of the day ahead. It was nearing the end of a difficult period in her life, and she was eager to share it with someone. But that was impossible, she sadly reminded herself.

Jennifer gave a small laugh as she dried herself off. She wasn't going to cry about it- she had come this far herself, and there was no turning back. She had to look forward.

Silently, she went back into the bedroom and looked for something to wear. She wanted to wear a blouse and a skirt that wouldn't be too warm. The June weather had brought unseasonably hot temperatures to Asheville and all of North Carolina. Finding a blue skirt and a white blouse, she finished dressing. Brushing her long hair back, she picked up a couple of notebooks and found her sunglasses. Getting ready now for the last two days of the college year, Jennifer Davis looked happily at a girlfriend she met as she walked down the hall to her class.

"Hi, Jennifer," Joyce called out to her.

"Hi, Joyce," she smiled.

As they went down the steps, Joyce asked her who was coming to see her graduate.

"I'll bet all your brothers and sisters and mom and dad will be here," Joyce enthused. "I know, even my grandparents are coming."

Jennifer shook her head.

"Nobody's going to be coming," she said quietly.

"Oh, that's too bad," Joyce exclaimed sadly.

As Joyce told her goodbye and hurried across the tree-shaded campus to her own class, once more, Jennifer Davis realized how truly alone she was in life.

She had enjoyed the benefits of being brought up in a wealthy family. The only drawback was that the material benefits her mother and father had provided for her could never compensate for the hollow feeling she felt inside as she recognized they had actually neglected her. No doubt, Father would send her a wire and promise her some money. Her mother would possibly phone and congratulate her. Jennifer Davis hurried to the auditorium where Eleanor Fitzgerald, the Dean of Luna Meadows College for Women, would give them the procedures for the graduation ceremony.

The auditorium was crowded, and everyone was talking. Apparently, a lot of the girls were chafing at the bit to be set free. As far as Jennifer Davis was concerned, she was becoming savagely angry. It gripped her mind to realize that she had made very few friends. After her roommate Susan Moore had gone on to New York City to work for a record company president, she had been left mostly alone. She hadn't heard from Susan in a while and now wished she had. But she was alone and wasn't going to worry about it.

Sitting in the back row, another girl asked, "Isn't it exciting? I mean, the graduation and the parties and everything."

"Oh, I guess so," Jennifer said quietly.

To herself, she was thinking she would survive. But it certainly was treacherous that her parents weren't there at the last lap. The Herculean efforts that had been required for her to get through college made her almost weak now as Jennifer realized that she apparently was alone.

Dead silence fell over the auditorium when Eleanor Fitzgerald went to the podium and began talking.

"Girls," she began seriously, "tomorrow is graduation day. And I want every one of you to make a good impression. Your caps and gowns are all here."

A sigh of relief seemed to rise from the auditorium as the girls looked at each other and contemplated the exciting moment when they would be dressed in a cap and gown, accepting their diplomas.

At this point, she explained the procedures for the graduation day and the reception to follow.

"This is a great triumph for all of you," Eleanor Fitzgerald smiled. "And it was worth the climb, wasn't it?"

The girls clapped, cheered, and applauded. However, Jennifer Davis couldn't bring herself to clap. In that awful instant, she realized that the effort hadn't been worth it.

"Aren't you excited?" the girl sitting beside Jennifer demanded.

"Yes, it's wonderful," she murmured, looking away.

Finally, the procedure sheets were passed out. Jennifer Davis looked the instructions over quickly, realizing graduation day was just another monotonous day as far as she was concerned.

2 – New York Calling

When Jennifer returned to her dormitory, she had a message waiting for her. Miss Jackson, who was in charge of the switchboard, called over to her.

"Jennifer," she smiled, waving a small pink paper, "you have a long-distance call."

"Long distance?" Jennifer asked in amazement. "I wonder who it could be."

Picking up the piece of paper, she read the name Susan Moore. Her roommate. She had remembered her! She was calling to congratulate her.

"Yes, yes, I'll take the call," she told her. "I'll go up to my room."

Once in her room, Jennifer opened the Venetian blinds and let the sunshine flood her room. Picking up the white phone near her bed, she dialed the operator. She gave her the number that Susan Moore had left, where she could be reached. Seconds later, Jennifer heard Susan's voice on the phone.

"Congratulations, Jennifer," Susan exclaimed excitedly, "I know how glad you are that you've made it."

"Thank you, Susan," Jennifer said quietly.

Before Jennifer could say anymore, Susan went on.

"I wanted to come out there and surprise you," she told her, "but I can't. We're having a big promotional appearance for our new rock star, Ziggy Falcon."

"You mean Ziggy Falcon is coming from London?"

"Yes," Susan enthused, "and we are going to give him a big welcome party to the Big Apple. John Williams, president of Empire Vinyl Records, has an exclusive contract with him."

"Oh, that sounds so exciting," Jennifer said, tears coming to her eyes as she realized she would be alone.

"I've got an idea," Susan enthused. "I haven't bought you a graduation gift yet. How would you like a ticket to the Big Apple?"

"What?" the words came tumbling out of Jennifer Davis' mouth as she suddenly realized what her girlfriend was suggesting.

"Yes," Susan insisted, "I want to buy you a plane ticket to New York City. You could skip the reception after your graduation and make it here just in time."

"That's true," Jennifer admitted gladly, "I could. It's earlier out there, isn't it?"

"Yes, you'll pick up time as you fly to our coast," Susan explained, "and all you'll have to do is graduate. If your folks treat you like they did the other years I was there, they won't show."

"You know, Mom and Dad," Jennifer said grimly.

"Oh, honey, there's so much to talk to you about," Susan bubbled, "I can hardly wait to see you."

"I haven't said I can come yet," Jennifer Davis insisted.

"But you've got to," Susan urged. "Please!"

All of a sudden, the world became beautiful. The sun was now rising in Jennifer's imagination as a blaze of glory tinted the clouds outside. It was beautiful. She could see the city. She could see Manhattan. The whole idea enchanted her.

"Are you going to take me up on my graduation gift?" Susan laughed.

"Yes, yes," Jennifer agreed excitedly. "It's wonderful of you to remember me."

"Remember you?" Susan said huskily. "Honey, I could never forget you. I just hoped that you hadn't forgotten me. There isn't anybody that... you know what I mean."

Jennifer Davis knew precisely what Susan Moore was talking about.

"There's nobody," she assured her, "and I'm dying to see you, too."

"Look, my boss is calling me," Susan apologized, "but I'm gonna send you that ticket. I'll wire it to you."

"Thanks," Jennifer told her gratefully. "Thanks so much for remembering me, Susan."

"Bye-bye, baby," Susan said as Jennifer said her goodbye.

Once she'd hung up the phone, Jennifer Davis stretched out on her bed. Dreamily, she closed her eyes. What had she to be afraid of? The future stretched out before her now. Destiny would take her to a new place, a new opportunity to make life rich and exciting. Her parents – what, did it matter? If they couldn't even bother to come and see her graduate, why should she bother to tell them about her plans?

Jennifer thought of all the packing she'd have to do, but she was up to it. Suddenly, doubts began surfacing in her mind. She couldn't just take a trip like that. It was a wild and wonderful idea, but it was completely impractical. What would happen once she got there? She didn't have any job. She only had three hundred dollars left in her savings account. And that wouldn't last for long. The more Jennifer Davis thought about it, the more unrealistic it seemed. She knew she would have to call Susan Moore and tell her she couldn't visit her. Sure, it would be fun, but she couldn't live just for a second. She had work to do. It hadn't been easy to get her degree. Bookkeeping was a difficult position. It had not been easy to acquire the knowledge and skills to make it possible for her to earn a high salary as a bookkeeper. She realized that more than anything else, she had to keep her balance now.

Getting up from the bed, Jennifer reached for the phone. She called Susan's number once more. Her girlfriend was surprised to hear her voice.

"What is it?" Susan asked.

"I've been thinking it over," Jennifer explained, "and I would love to come to New York, but I have to think of a job. I... I appreciate you want to send me the money for the ticket, but it's more than that."

"What is it?" Susan asked nervously.

"I've worked hard to get my degree," Jennifer tried to explain. "You've got to understand. I have to think of a job."

"Honey," Susan told her, "I was going to surprise you. There's an opening for a bookkeeper at Empire Vinyl Records. And that was why I wanted you to come here."

Jennifer Davis was grateful that Susan had been thinking in practical terms.

"That's wonderful," she told her. "It really is. That was what I was so worried about. All right, I'll do it."

With a smile now, Jennifer put the phone down after she thanked Susan again. It was going to be a difficult move. She had never been to New York before, and it would be a different kind of life. But it would be a good move. North Carolina had been so dreadfully hot last summer that she was anxious to get the cooler climate and wear fashionable clothes.

Going over to the closet, she opened the sliding glass mirrored doors. She looked at all of her clothes. Jennifer had been so busy with her college work that she hadn't left herself much time to think about buying new clothes. But she wouldn't worry about it. The important thing now was preparing for the graduation ceremony the following day.

A few moments later, there was a knock on the door. Her girlfriend from down the hall was visiting her.

"Oh, Joyce, come on in," Jennifer invited her. Joyce was a beautiful redhead. She was wearing a pink cotton blouse and a blue denim skirt.

"Aren't you excited?" Joyce enthused. "I mean, tomorrow, and it's all over. We can begin living."

"Yes," Jennifer told her, "I am excited. I'm going to New York."

Joyce was amazed to hear her say this.

"You never mentioned that before," she told her. "What happened?"

"A friend of mine," Jennifer Davis said protectively, "has invited me. I'm going to work out there. Isn't that exciting?"

"Yes," Joyce told her, "I guess you've been holding out on me. You have a boyfriend up north."

Jennifer laughed.

"Joyce, why do you always read something into everything?"

Joyce smiled and explained, "Well, why else would you go there?"

Jennifer knew she must say nothing, for it would be dreadful if Joyce ever suspected that she and Susan Moore had been carrying on.

"I've got a lot of packing to do, Joyce," she excused herself. "I hope you don't mind."

Shaking her head, Joyce told her no.

"You've got to keep in touch," she urged her.

"I'll see you later. Remember, we have to practice in the auditorium at four this afternoon."

"I won't forget," Jennifer assured her.

Once she was gone, Jennifer had time to think. She remembered all too vividly how her mother and father had stayed together because of their financial situation. Her mother had constantly badgered her with her problems. And the problems were still unsolved. Her mother was saying she might have done better if she had married a doctor. Jennifer was certain that her mother had fallen in love with a doctor friend of hers.

Her father had become involved with a secretary who worked for him. Even though she was certain the secretary was acting as his mistress, Jennifer would never say anything. She figured that he had a perfect right to do as he felt he should. However, she wanted to do as she felt she should with her own life. The advances that many men had made toward her in the past had been disgusting and repellent as far as Jennifer was concerned. She had a beautiful body that could turn any man on. Even though many men had tried to get it off with her, she had managed to elude them.

A laugh, a smile, and a gentle shove had managed to keep her from getting intimately involved with any of them. It had come as quite a surprise that Susan Moore had wanted to have sex with her. Certainly, she had heard of such things, but she always pictured lesbians as rather masculine women.

Yet Susan Moore was a stunning brunette with a shapely form that had many men panting after her. It was quite a jolting surprise the first time Susan had smiled at Jennifer's naked body when she emerged from a shower. She was standing there with the water still on her body as she reached for a towel. However, Susan had become so awed by her naked beauty that she didn't want her to move. She had told her that she was a statue and should be carved in marble to retain her beauty for posterity. Jennifer Davis had broken up laughing. She had thought Susan was kidding. However, she soon discovered she wasn't kidding at all when she suggested they have sex together!

It had been difficult for Jennifer to accept her roommate's advances, but she had finally agreed to lie down on the bed and allow Susan to make passionate love to her. Yet she had somehow enjoyed it, and that was the exciting part. Susan's dreamy brown eyes looking at her crotch so tenderly and her pink tongue sliding along her vagina had excited Jennifer. It was strange how delicious and stimulating it could be to have sex with someone who was so gentle.

She loved the way Susan would let her hands roam over her naked body. It was stimulating when Susan would suck on her bosoms and gently nibble on them. Was that why Susan wanted her to come to New York? She had asked her if she had any serious attachment. Very likely, Susan was thinking of her sexually. But it didn't bother Jennifer. After all, only this morning, as she had played with herself, she was thinking of Susan's hot tongue stabbing in her pussy. It would have been so erotically satisfying.

There wasn't anything wrong with a woman making love to another woman. How could a man possibly appreciate her body the way a woman could? She reasoned.

Jennifer knew she had to be quick and efficient. She started to select the dresses that she wanted to take with her. Some clothes were so dated that she would give them away. Absent-mindedly, she pulled the dresses from the closet and tossed them on the bed. One pile of clothes would be the rejects; the others would be the ones to accompany her on her Big Apple hop.

Jennifer was thinking about the jet trip as she segregated and packed clothes. She had never traveled that far. Sure, she had gone on small trips, but never anything this big. And to think of leaving the security of the ivy-covered buildings at Luna Meadows College for Women made her feel sad and lonely. She had to erase these thoughts from her mind. The illusions of living in the past could only leave a certain amount of depression. She had to live for the future, yet she hoped that New York would provide the beautiful surrounding atmosphere that would refresh her and excite her to enjoy life the way she knew it should be.

The past year had been lonely without Susan. But all that would be changed now.

It was amazing to Jennifer how many things she had collected that she didn't want anymore. The small plastic wastebasket in the corner of the bedroom could never hold all of the items she had to throw away. She knew she would have to get boxes and fill them to overflowing, yet it would be worth it. For in just two days, she would be seeing Susan Moore again. And the thought of seeing Susan made her heart leap with joy.

Hurrying down to the college bookstore, a young man helped her with the boxes.

"Looks like you're really moving," he smiled.

"I am," Jennifer agreed. "I'm going to New York!"

3 – The Performance

Jennifer had become so concerned with packing and preparing for the trip that she was late for the afternoon rehearsal at the auditorium. Elgar's Pomp and Circumstances could be heard wafting on the summer breeze as she entered the auditorium. Looking around the room, she observed shafts of afternoon light filtering through the Gothic-styled windows. She remembered vividly how many times she had listened to Eleanor Fitzgerald give the girls admonitions about their future careers. In a way, she was sorry it was over. The security that she'd experienced here at Luna Meadows College for Women could not be dealt with lightly.

Walking to her place in line, she noticed the eagle eye of Eleanor Fitzgerald looking directly at her. It made her feel awkward and nervous.

After the rehearsal for the graduation ceremonies, Jennifer went to the nearby college coffee shop. To her surprise, she ran into Michael Johnson. Michael held her arm as he greeted her warmly.

"What are you doing tonight?" he smiled.

"Please, Michael," she shook her head, "I'm busy packing."

"Maybe we can go somewhere together this weekend," he told her. "We'll both be back in Charlotte."

"I won't be," she told him, her eyes strained. "I'm going North."

"What?" Michael asked, looking at her in amazement as he rubbed his fingers through his hair.

"Yes, I'm going to New York," she said quietly.

His hand came under her chin, and she could feel the coolness of his expression as he gazed into her eyes.

"Have a good time," he told her.

It bothered her that Michael was acting like this. She never did care for him, and when he came on strong like this, she cared for him even less.

"You're gonna miss me," he told her emphatically.

He was smiling down at her with an expression that rocked her heart. Michael was so tall, so dear, with his dark head silhouetted against the darkened night sky that as she looked up at him, she wanted to put her arms around him for a moment. Instead, she smiled heroically and told him, "I've got to go where the job is. I've been offered a position in New York City."

Michael shook his head.

"Come on and sit down," he told her. "I want to talk to you."

He led her inside the coffee shop, and she sank down on a wooden chair. Michael didn't sit beside her but pulled a chair up from the other side of the table where she was seated.

She looked at his rather stem profile as he gazed into her eyes.

"You always said you were too busy," he reminded her, "to go out much with me. I was looking forward to getting acquainted with you in Charlotte."

It bothered him that Jennifer acted ambivalent. She was

indifferent one moment and then looking up at him as if she liked him the next. Her heart lurched near her throat as she realized she did sort of like him.

"I have to do this," she said weakly.

"I guess you do," Michael frowned, "and you don't care much about me."

He straightened up in his chair when the waitress came and took his order. After the coffee had been brought to their table, she tried to explain her view to him.

"I've never been too happy at home. I've got to go where I think I will enjoy my life more."

Michael's frown disappeared, and he gave a smile.

"All right," he told her, "if that's what you want, that's what you want."

She was careful not to do anything that would upset him further. She recognized very well that he really did like her. Yet it was apparent to her that their relationship could never come to anything.

"I'll survive," he said with a small smile.

After coffee, he walked her back to her dormitory.

"Take care," Michael told her.

She nodded and thanked him, then went up to her room alone.

That night, she was thinking. It was difficult to get to sleep. There was so much that still had to be done. She had a small bank account that she would have to concern herself with. There wouldn't be enough time tomorrow to take care of that. She would have to write from New York to the bank and have them send the money to her there.

She recognized that it would be only fair to tell her father where she was. When she called his number late that night, the exchange answered. She simply left a message that she was going to New York for a job following graduation. She concluded that he would contact her if her father cared at all about her. But she doubted very much he would. As far as her mother was concerned, she was seldom home, and she wouldn't bother leaving her a message. She knew she would object to her making such a distant move and didn't want to clash with her.

Finally, she showered and prepared for bed. Sleeping in the nude was her custom, and tonight, as she pulled the sheets over her naked body, she couldn't help but think of her girlfriend. It heated her loins just imagining Susan making love to her. Sex was something that she hadn't had for one year. Ever since Susan had graduated and gone to Manhattan to work as a secretary for the president of a large rock and roll record company, she had been frustrated and had done a lot of masturbating. But all of this would come to an end when she met Susan again. She knew very well how much Susan had loved her. She could almost see her hot eyes gazing at her naked body.

Drifting off to a sound sleep, she didn't hear a thing until the next morning when the shrill sound of the alarm clock awakened her. She had to get up around seven as the graduation was set for ten-fifteen.

There wasn't much more packing to do, but Jennifer made sure everything was done. Once more, she had to throw a lot of things away that she couldn't use. She wanted to put them in boxes, but she'd run out of them, so she simply placed them on the floor in the corner with a note to the house mother.

Going to the auditorium at nine-thirty, she slipped into her graduation robe and cap. The strains of Pomp And Circumstance made her remember Susan Moore's graduation ceremony. Recalling how much she missed Susan and how painful it was to see her march down the aisle to pick up her degree, she knew they would be separated. And it was this separation that had bothered her. However, the thought of now being reunited with Susan excited and delighted Jennifer.

The graduation services were painful in some ways and pleasurable in others. Her eyes looked around the auditorium to see if she could locate her mother or father. When she didn't see either one of them, it troubled her. As the parents and friends went around the line of graduates to congratulate them, the keen disappointment of being left alone once more bothered Jennifer. She lowered her eyes as she realized she was totally by herself.

It didn't hurt her to leave the line very early.

Explaining her reason for leaving early to Eleanor Fitzgerald, who was standing by and watching everything, she was pleased there were no objections.

The last lap was over. Now she had to hurry and get her luggage so she could catch a taxi to the airport. The ticket Susan Moore had wired to her had been brought to her room at the graduation ceremonies. This had bothered her as she didn't want any hitches.

Picking up her ticket and slipping into a jacket, she took

her two heavy pieces of luggage and struggled with them down the steps to the waiting taxi outside.

The taxi driver sped her to the airport. She sighed with weary relief as she boarded the plane and handed the airline stewardess her ticket. It was wonderful that she had finally made it.

Once on the plane, she leaned back and relaxed. The meal was served when they were in the air, but Jennifer didn't care to eat. She wanted to sleep.

Almost before she knew it, the soaring aircraft was swooping down the city of New York. She looked out the window beside her and saw the mountains surrounding the city. The impressive skyline was a pleasant contrast to the hazy day she had left behind in North Carolina. As the plane landed on the runway and the brakes were applied, a sudden jolt of the reality of what was happening to her seemed to pierce through Jennifer's consciousness completely now. She had left her parents thousands of miles away and was beginning her life anew. It wouldn't be easy.

After she had disembarked, she went to wait for her luggage at the front of the John F. Kennedy International Airport. She didn't see Susan Moore anywhere. This bothered her. Finally, her luggage came along, and she reached out to pull it from the rotating luggage rack.

Carrying her luggage to where the yellow taxis were waiting, she suddenly spotted Susan Moore. Susan didn't look the same at all. She had a completely different hairdo, and her clothes were so modern.

"Oh, honey, I'm sorry," Susan apologized, "I got caught in traffic on the Parkway. You don't know how bad traffic is here."

As she looked into Susan's eyes, Jennifer felt hot tears stain her cheeks.

"Aren't you glad to see me?" Susan grinned, knowing full well why she was crying.

"Yes, yes," Jennifer exclaimed, throwing her arms around her.

The two college roommates hugged, and then Susan led her to a black limousine parked at the curb. A black chauffeur opened the door for them.

"Is this yours?" Jennifer asked in amazement.

"Well, it's the company's," Susan smiled proudly, "but I can use it. It's very convenient to have a driver in this city."

As the limousine smoothly navigated through the bustling streets of New York City, weaving its way amidst the towering skyscrapers and vibrant sidewalks, Jennifer gazed out in awe. The city's skyline, a majestic tapestry of architectural wonders, rose high above them, casting its grandeur against the backdrop of a clear sky. The sun, setting amidst the urban landscape, bathed the buildings in a golden hue, making the scene even more breathtaking.

"It's so interesting here," Jennifer exclaimed, her eyes wide with admiration as she saw the skyscrapers gleaming in the sunlight and the busy sidewalks teeming with life.

"I love it, too," Susan agreed, sharing in her friend's excitement as she peered out at the bustling city streets, where the energy of New York was palpable.

When they finally arrived at Susan's high-rise apartment

building in the heart of the city, Jennifer's excitement was palpable.

"Wow," she said to her friend, her voice filled with wonder, "it's beautiful here."

The limousine came to a halt by the sidewalk, right in front of the rather rundown entrance in the Upper West Side. Susan quickly stepped out to assist Jennifer with her luggage, their eyes sparkling from the enchanting cityscape they had just traversed.

"Honey," she told her, "we've got to get you some new clothes. We're having a big party tonight. Empire Vinyl Records has invited Ziggy Falcon here from London. And this will be his introduction to the United States fans. He's performing at Radio City Music Hall. After that, we're going to hold a party at the company offices on Park Avenue."

"Oh, it all sounds so exciting," Jennifer exclaimed.

Once she had brought her luggage into the two-bed apartment, Susan Moore helped her unpack.

"You really do need some different clothes," she told her as she surveyed the wardrobe Jennifer had brought with her.

Jennifer was looking at Susan Moore with obvious admiration. It was apparent that her clothes matched the style in NYC. And it bothered Jennifer that she didn't have any clothes like this.

"I... I really need to go shopping," Jennifer told her.

"There's a beautiful boutique not far from here," she assured her. "Let's get back into Manhattan."

Looking at her watch, Jennifer agreed that they would have to hurry as time was running out.

Just before the little shop closed in Soho, Susan managed to find some mod clothes for Jennifer.

"What about your hair?" she shook her head. "We've got to do something about it."

A small hair stylist's shop across from the boutique was open. Susan Moore usually got what she wanted, and now was an opportunity to prove how effective she could be in getting people to do what she wanted. Her lively mind and interest were caught up by the beautiful wardrobe that she'd helped Jennifer purchase. But she was also eager to see to it that her hair looked as attractive as possible.

"Over there," she told her, "a lot of famous people have their hair done. You just don't wear your hair long like that anymore. We'll get it taken care of, don't you worry."

Together, the two girls went into the posh hair salon. Susan Moore had a talent for giving the impression of being a very important person, and when Marco Valentino approached the two young women, he looked at Jennifer with some amusement, knowing full well that she would be one to need his services.

"What's the problem?" the young hairstylist smiled.

"I want you to help her," Susan said anxiously. "We're going to meet some very important people tonight. She just flew in from the South, so if you could fix her up with the latest hairdo to fit her face the best, I'd make it worth your while."

Marco Valentino looked at Jennifer for a long moment.

"You're not giving me much time," he shook his head.

"But you can perform miracles," Susan Moore smiled.

Her cunning and her charm captivated Marco, who nodded.

"All right," he told her, drawn by her courteous manner and her obvious admiration for his skill.

Marco Valentino studied Susan Davis for a long moment as she sat in the chair in front of the mirror. He paid a lot of attention to her unique bone structure.

"You're a very lovely girl," he told her. "You're the type of good-looking girl that could attract any man."

Susan Moore did not appreciate the unexpected comment. She wanted Marco to pay attention to his task and not become absorbed with Jennifer Davis' beauty. She was all too aware of what a lovely, sensuous girl Jennifer Davis was.

"All right," he told Jennifer, "I'll take care of giving you a fresh New York look." Looking at Susan, he added, "If you want to come back in a little while, I can work with her alone."

Susan recognized a sudden surge of anger. He was suggesting that she shouldn't superimpose her idea of what constituted a good hairdo for Jennifer. She almost trembled with anger, but she controlled herself by pressing her lips together and looking at him in a self-righteous manner.

"I think I know what would suit her best," she told him firmly.

"Don't take it so seriously," Marco said evenly. "You're a lovely girl, Susan, and I enjoy fixing your hair. But let me decide on what would look best for Jennifer."

Even though Susan Moore silently felt it was terribly unfair for her not to be able to contribute her viewpoints on what would make Jennifer's hairdo more attractive, she decided it was best to leave. She shrugged and pretended she didn't care.

"All right, I could pick up a few things," she told him as she smiled down at Jennifer tolerantly.

Marco Valentino didn't take long to decide what would frame Jennifer Davis' face correctly. Jennifer was pleased to see how eager he was to help her.

"Now," he told her quietly, "if you would just relax, it will come out right."

When Susan Moore returned about forty-five minutes later, she was delighted. Jennifer Davis had an ethereal look. Marco had given her a special cut. It was surprising to her that she could look so lovely with shorter hair. The crimpled hairstyle that Jennifer now wore gave her a very sensuous appeal as well. Marco couldn't restrain complimenting her.

"You have an enchanting color to your hair," he told Jennifer, "and it's natural."

It pleased her that he had done so much to bring out her charm and beauty.

With new clothes that they had purchased, Susan and Jennifer quickly got the subway back up to the Upper West Side again.

"We'll just have time for a drink, get dressed, and get to the show," Susan told Jennifer.

Once more, they hurried in and got dressed. When Susan looked at Jennifer's body as she stripped, she realized once more what a beautiful figure her girlfriend possessed.

"You don't even need a brassiere," she told her as she looked at her firm young breasts. "They stand up magnificently."

Coming over to her for a moment, she gently caressed her bosoms.

"I wish we had time now," she whispered sensuously as she glanced down at her crotch. "But that will have to come later."

Putting her arms around her, she kissed her tenderly. She felt the warmth of Jennifer Davis' bosoms as she wrapped her arms tightly to her. After a lengthy, passionate kiss, the two girls hurriedly prepared to go to the evening's concert.

Going to the kitchen, Susan prepared drinks. They sat on the sofa, looking at the brick wall of the building opposite.

"I'll bet you love it out here," Jennifer told her.

"Yes, except for the crime," Susan laughed. "But I have been lucky. But the neighbor wasn't so lucky. Now he has nothing."

"What do you mean?"

"He was robbed," Susan said sadly, "of everything he had."

Looking at her diamond-studded watch, Susan suggested they had better hurry.

Once more, they hurried down to the subway heading south.

"These trains," Susan shook her head, "they wear me out."

Jennifer smiled at her.

"But you love it," she assured her. "That's why you wanted me to come out here, isn't it?"

Susan nodded.

"I do have an exciting life," she agreed. "It is wonderful to be in the music industry."

"I hear a lot of people in this business are on dope," Jennifer said to her, wondering if she would reveal much about what she might know.

"Don't believe everything you hear," she said, smiling at her. "But if you want any grass, honey, I've got some of the best."

Jennifer had never smoked grass and wasn't about to start now. It surprised her that Susan was so bold in making a suggestion like this.

"You do smoke grass, don't you?" Susan asked her.

Jennifer shook her head. "I... I haven't tried any," she said nervously, hoping Susan wouldn't pursue that any further.

When they got up on the street, Jennifer attracted the attention of a group of young men.

"Wow!" one boy exclaimed. "Get a load of that."

Susan smiled pleasantly as she looked at Jennifer.

"You see," she told her, "it's having an effect already. That new hairdo and that pink dress really do wonders for you."

At this point, she was keenly aware that Susan was watching every aspect of her life. Susan's eyes were preoccupied with her, and it excited her. They found their seats close to the front of the Radio City Music Hall stage. It was amazing how huge the building was. The classic design appealed to Jennifer. The indirect floodlighting, which created patterns of light and shadow around the circular building, impressed her enormously.

"What a fantastic place," Jennifer exclaimed, "and all this space. It's so different from back in North Carolina."

The crowds were packing the place, and police security guards were strong in evidence.

"I never realized how popular Ziggy Falcon was," Jennifer admitted.

"He's sensational," Susan assured her, "and his records are going to clobber the competition. John Williams, the boss, is really high on this guy."

It appeared that Empire Vinyl Records had another winner. However, Jennifer was so amazed at everything happening to her that she could hardly collect her senses. She had gone through an agony of longing for Susan Moore. And seeing the tender smile on her face now, she wanted to tell her the truth that she loved her. But she didn't know if her girlfriend still felt the same way about her. This bothered her.

"Are you glad I came?" Jennifer asked quietly.

"You know I am," Susan replied huskily as they found their seats and sat down.

It wasn't long before the crowd's agitation had become a chant.

"We want Ziggy," they called out across the footlights. "We want Ziggy!"

Then, the rock star appeared like a blinding light in the center of the stage. The loud rock music thundered through the Hall as the audience stood and cheered wildly. It was the moment they had all waited for. John Williams and all of the people who worked at Empire Vinyl Records were there watching with delight.

"Wow!" Susan exclaimed excitedly. "They really love him."

When Ziggy Falcon realized how wild the audience was, he spoke slowly, aware of a sudden trembling.

"I knew a few of you had heard about me," he began quietly, "but I didn't think you were going to welcome me like this."

He made a gesture of gratitude, and the audience went wild.

"Ziggy, Ziggy," they thundered, requesting different songs that he had made famous.

Susan Moore was high. She was turning around to watch the excited expressions of the audience. Then she looked over at John Williams, who was seated not far from her. John was watching her, his heart leaping with excitement as he saw the passionate frenzy that had devoured the crowd when Ziggy Falcon stepped on the stage.

Finally, the audience quieted and sat down silently. Ziggy Falcon was the great entertainer they always expected him to be. He proved he could milk the audience of every emotion. Using his arms, his dancing skill, and his powerful singing vibrations, he twisted their ears and minds until they were cheering for him in thunderous applause.

"He's really going over big," Susan exclaimed delightedly.

After the intermission and the concert continued, Jennifer looked at Susan. She was somewhat bewildered. Susan was not the girl that she'd known in college. She had changed. It was obvious that she had entered a completely new world. It was equally obvious that their relationship could never be the same again. Jennifer found it troubling just thinking about it.

"I'm so glad you're here," Susan whispered during a lush love song that Ziggy Falcon had slowed down to sing.

Jennifer reached out and held Susan's hand. However, Susan pulled away.

"Not here, honey," she giggled. "Somebody from the office might get the right idea if you know what I mean."

There was lustful desire lurking behind the gleam in Susan's eyes, which Jennifer could easily define. Something that made her tingle and sparkle like champagne. She was anxious to make Susan happy, and she felt so lucky that she could be looking at her teasingly now, saying nothing but feeling everything. She knew that she was anxious to eat her up, and she could hardly wait for that approaching moment when the two of them would be naked together in bed. It was terrible to be tortured like this when she wanted her so much.

Susan Moore listened solemnly to the great rock star as he wrung every emotion in the book from his audience, holding them in the palm of his hand. All of his stage actions had been deliberate, and he knew exactly how to use his hands, arms, feet, eyes, and voice. It was total entertainment. Every part of him was working toward the hypnotism that he was performing so effectively now.

When the accompanying rock band blared, and his voice echoed throughout the great Music Hall, the audience once more was howling and on its feet. After a standing ovation of over ten minutes, Ziggy Falcon stood there tired, his lips trembling and tears in his eyes.

"Wow!" he exclaimed. "You sure made this a great day for me."

Ziggy's smile looked so sincere, so boyishly endearing, that his heart reached out to everyone.

"I'm afraid you'll spoil me," he told his captive audience.

The mesmerized crowd loved to hear him talk as he

effectively spun his stage magic about them. When the evening concert was over, he simply grinned at them and told them the entire concert would be put on the Empire Vinyl Record label. This made John Williams so delighted he jumped to his feet, clasping his hand like a boxing champ in the ring's corner. It made Susan Moore bend over in laughter.

"What are you laughing at?" Jennifer Davis asked, unaware of the strange byplay between the rock star and the record promoter.

"Look over there," Susan smiled. "Take a look at John. He's getting convulsions."

Looking at the expression on John's face, it did appear that he was having convulsions. Money convulsions. He could see the cash register ringing every time Ziggy Falcon was singing on an Empire Vinyl Record label.

Once the noise crowd had dispersed, Jennifer Davis felt she and Susan could be together.

"I'm so anxious to be with you – alone," Jennifer whispered.

"We will be, darling," Susan smiled back softly, "but right now, we have to go to the big party at the office. We're celebrating Ziggy Falcon's bow in Manhattan."

Jennifer Davis' smile was wistful.

"I can't believe it's all happening," she said as Susan drove down the freeway again. "It's like a crazy dream, but I know it's true... thanks to you. It was so sweet of you to send me the ticket to come here."

"You liked that?"

Jennifer nodded affectionately.

"It was really sweet of you. Nobody did anything for me but you."

Susan Moore was fully aware of the neglect of her parents. It pleased her that she could pull up the slack, and she did it for her own reasons.

"Where on earth are we going?" Jennifer asked curiously as they hopped into a cab. She was amazed at how large New York City was.

"We are on our way to our offices on Park and 59th Street," Susan explained. "It's not far from Central Park, but we'll have to explore that another day."

"Central Park?" Jennifer echoed. "I saw a movie about that once. I know what that is."

"Right on," Susan assured her, "and that's where Empire Vinyl has its record headquarters."

"Oh, it's so exciting," Jennifer observed as they drove up Park Avenue.

The towering skyscrapers of Manhattan seemed to sweep by them as the car headed forward.

"What impressive buildings," Jennifer observed. "I've never seen anything like it."

They finally came to the towering office building where Empire Vinyl had its headquarters.

"That's where we are," Susan told Jennifer proudly, pointing at the massive steel and smoked glass building.

"What a view they must have from there," Jennifer observed as she struggled to see the top floors.

"You can see Central Park from there," Susan assured her.

Susan paid the cabbie, and they left and took the elevator to the thirty-first floor.

"This is what I call class," Jennifer told her honestly.

"Yes, we really do have a posh suite for our headquarters. But Empire Vinyl has some of the best rock stars in the world under contract, so I guess we deserve the best."

They exited the elevator and walked down the thickly carpeted hallway to the Empire Vinyl Records' modernistic offices. Opening the door, Jennifer could see the party had already begun inside. Crowds of people were talking, and the waiters were carrying silver trays with drinks around the room.

"We couldn't even get into Radio City Music Hall," a secretary shook her head as she walked toward Susan.

"Oh, Patricia, that's too bad," Susan shook her head. "But I thought everyone here had tickets."

"We did," Patricia explained, "but somebody figured out a way to make copies of the tickets, so a lot of people were shut out. It was a bad scene."

"That's pretty awful," Susan shook her head. "I've heard of people making counterfeit money but never of counterfeit tickets."

"It just shows how popular Ziggy Falcon is," Patricia smiled. "I guess Empire Vinyl is really going to make a mint on him."

Going over to the bar, Susan ordered a drink for herself.

"What are you going to have, Jennifer?" she asked. Jennifer ordered a Brandy Alexander, and the two girls went over to the windows overlooking the city of New York spread out below. The lights of the city twinkled brightly in a blazing panorama before them. Jennifer could hardly believe she was here in Manhattan, attending a party for the hottest rock recording star in the business. What a fantastic future lay before her, she thought to herself. She truly was starting a new life.

4 – On TU

A handsome young Latino waiter came by, carrying a silver tray on which were many crystal goblets. Putting her Brandy Alexander aside, Jennifer reached for a champagne glass.

"I'd love this," she smiled.

Noticing how much she was enjoying herself, Susan smiled.

"How's this for a graduation party?" she grinned at her.

"Oh, it's been wonderful," Jennifer enthused, "it really has. I can't thank you enough, Susan."

A moment later, another waiter came by carrying hors d'oeuvres. The large shrimps, the lobster, and the small, dainty, open-faced sandwiches appealed to her.

"Frankly, I'm starved," she admitted candidly. "I didn't feel like eating on the plane. I slept almost all of the way here."

Seconds later, the tall, dark, and handsome John Williams strode into the main reception room. Everyone applauded as John entered.

"Enough, enough," John waved as he walked over to Susan. "I'm so glad you all had a good time."

Susan was eager to introduce Jennifer to her boss.

"John, I want you to meet Jennifer," Susan smiled as she introduced herself.

John looked at Jennifer as if he were undressing her. She was conscious of his dark eyes staring at her bosoms, and now she wished she'd worn a bra beneath the clinging pink fabric of her dress. Susan told her that girls in New York didn't wear bras, particularly under the type of clinging dress she wore that evening.

"Hello," John grinned in a friendly, sexy manner, apparently pleased at what he saw.

"I'm so happy to be here," Jennifer assured him. "It was really great seeing Ziggy Falcon tonight."

"Ziggy's going to be with us a little later," John assured her.

At that point, John told Susan he wanted to talk to her. Jennifer assumed it was about the business as Susan had revealed she was John's private secretary.

"I'll see you later, honey," Susan smiled as she and John left the main office and went into his private office.

Jennifer walked over to one of the waiters and took another long-stemmed goblet of champagne from the sparkling silver tray. At that point, she noticed two young men setting up a large-screened television set.

"What's happening?" she asked curiously.

"We're going to show the rock show on our own closed-circuit television," he explained. "We videotaped it tonight."

Jennifer Davis was pleased and excited to think she would see it all over again. Going over to the window, she looked at the twinkling lights of the city of Manhattan, which sparkled like diamonds against a black velvet background. Out there somewhere lay her destiny, her future! It was strange how much it looked at this point, like Charlotte, North Carolina. She remembered the Top of the Sixes and how much she enjoyed the view of the city from there. She thought that all big cities looked alike if you were high enough to catch a perspective of the lights shimmering far down below in the darkness of night.

Just then, she heard the loud rock beat as Ziggy Falcon's face flashed on the television screen. The lights were lowered, and everyone paid close attention.

Jennifer thought she saw Ziggy Falcon slipping into the room quietly, but she wasn't certain. However, she kept looking out of the corner of her eye as she went on watching the television screen. The large screen provided a perfect opportunity to see every detail of the rock star's super performance. Going to get some more champagne, she spotted Ziggy Falcon. He looked at her hungrily.

"Hi," he smiled.

It was strange, but Jennifer didn't reply. This intrigued Ziggy as he was used to having women fall all over him. Going to a corner of the room where she could have that fantastic view of the lights of Manhattan, she would glance out the window one moment and look back at the screen another. However, the closed-circuit television had been left on in John Williams's private office unbeknownst to him. When the rock concert had finished, suddenly there was a hush as everyone looked at the screen and saw what was happening in the next room.

Immediately, Jennifer saw what kind of business John Williams wanted to discuss with her girlfriend, Susan Moore. She gasped aloud, her eyes glued to the unbelievable sex action unfolding on the huge screen. There was Susan, stark naked. She was walking toward John with a pleased smile on her face.

"I've got a big one for you, baby," John grinned at her, his voice coming through the speakers loud and clear.

Walking over to him, Susan gripped his huge, throbbing penis. He smiled with complete satisfaction as she fondled his long, hard cock. Jennifer Davis' mind reeled as she recognized the endless trail of frustration she had created for herself by coming to New York. She had imagined that Susan Moore was so crazy about her that she wouldn't have sex with anyone else. After all, she had sent her a ticket. She couldn't understand why she would do something like this.

She blushed as she watched the screen until she was a bright crimson color. She shook her head and looked away. And then, as she heard people laughing, she looked once more to see what was happening on the closed-circuit television screen.

At this point, she was jacking him off.

"It's really long and hard, honey," Susan smiled as the sound amplified over the closed-circuit television.

It made Jennifer want to wretch. After all, it was like sticking a dagger in her heart. Susan certainly ought to be told what was happening. The wrong switch had inadvertently been turned on through a foul-up in the television circuit panel, letting everything in John Williams' office come over on the closed-circuit TV that the entire office force was gazing at so anxiously.

All at once, Jennifer Davis' eyes were drawn to John's virile erection. It was as if she was compelled with a burning urge to watch, no matter how much she hated it. However, it was obvious Susan Moore either enjoyed what she was doing with her boss enormously or was putting on an Academy Award performance.

Susan's hands grasped the quivering, huge, blue-veined thickness of John's naked, stiff erection.

"Do you like it, Susan honey?" John Williams whispered loud enough for everyone in the office to hear on closed-circuit TV.

"Hhhmm, yes," she told him huskily, her naked breasts rising and falling anxiously.

"Go ahead and rub it," John told Susan, "rub my nuts, too, while you're at it. Better yet, baby, kiss it."

Her hand jerked away, but his grip on her wrist kept her fingers close to the turgid heat of his stiffened cock. He pulled her hand back to it and made her close her palm once more around the pulsating warmth of his long, throbbing cock.

"That's how honey," he smirked.

John's other hand grabbed her shoulder and squeezed. "Why don't you give it a little nibble just to show me you mean business, baby?" he urged.

Jennifer Davis' eyes widened with fear. She didn't want to see her girlfriend going down on John Williams. Emotions of frustration, confusion, and jealousy surged through her now as she watched the erotic spectacle in living color on the large television screen.

"Come on, baby," John told his secretary anxiously, "we haven't got all night. They're probably wondering what we're doing out there."

That brought laughter to everyone in the room. The waiters were so amused that they stood there dead in their tracks, just watching, not taking the champagne to anyone. But it didn't matter much, as nobody was drinking. They were all too busy watching what was happening in the next room.

John pushed harder at Susan's shoulder, forcing her to kneel obediently in front of him. As she dropped to her knees, she looked up and seemed to tremble with fear and remorse. Jennifer was certain that Susan didn't enjoy this. She realized that she obviously had made a big mistake in coming here. It got her angry and upset to see poor Susan forced to endure such torture. Susan looked up, her eyes revealing her shame as she gazed at the naked boss's cock. Jennifer had to tell herself the truth.

Why didn't she go in there and let Susan know what was happening? The burning pain of her own long, unsatisfied desires ached now between Jennifer's warm, supple thighs like the throbbing hurt of a pulled muscle. She could feel the fast-spreading dampness of her passion, and her panties stuck wetly to the soft hair-fringed lips of her pussy as she tried desperately to forget the urges within her for Susan to love her.

Frowning down at her through the narrow slits of his eyes, John declared, "Susan, baby, you've got me all heated up like this. Now come on and put up, or I'll get rough with you."

The people who were watching the erotic action on the television screen all burst out laughing. However, it was no laughing matter for the lonely girl Jennifer Davis, who stood there watching her female lover have to do degrading acts for her boss. She was trembling with outrage. At this point, she was so concerned with what was happening that she continued keeping her eyes glued to the large TV screen, watching with avid interest like everyone else in the office.

"Please, John," Susan begged, "I'm making a mistake coming into your office now. I'm sorry." Her eyes were reddened with shame as she peered up at her naked boss. Susan was telling the truth. However, she knew there was a burning desire within her own loins. She could feel the fast-spreading dampness of her passion.

"I want you to go down on me," John frowned.

At this point, he grabbed her head.

"Don't bother me with all this crap. Suck my cock, baby. Suck my prick and suck it good."

He jokingly raised his fist to her head. However, Jennifer wasn't so sure that he might not hit her if she didn't comply. The fierce gleam of hostility surfaced in his stare. He changed in seconds to a smiling, handsome man, glowering threateningly down at Susan. She was helpless to resist.

"Grab it," he demanded, "and put it in your mouth."

She was closer now to the tip of his mammoth cock. A crystal bead of cum dripped from its tip as she slowly opened her mouth. The lascivious act that he wanted her to perform bothered her. All at once John's fingers twisted cruelly in her hair, and he suddenly tightened his grip until a handful of her hair was in his hand as he pulled her to his penis.

"Now," he demanded, "open your mouth."

John thrust his hairy pelvis forward a few inches, and the bulbous, purplish head of his circumcised prick slithered over her trembling lips and into the warm sanctuary of her mouth.

"Hmm, no," she begged, gagging at the hugeness of his

erection, but it was too late. His cock was buried deeply in her mouth now, and he had savored the warm wetness of her saliva as her tongue moistened his cock.

There was no stopping John now.

"Real nice, Susan, just lick it like that. Yes, honey, that's what I need to get the party really rolling. A good cock-sucking."

He held her head with both hands now and was working her face back and forth onto the thick, blood-heated flesh of his erection. Susan managed to keep her tongue away from it for a few seconds, but it was a useless struggle. Furthermore, she quickly discovered that the taste was delicious, not like she had remembered from the couple of times she and John had half-heartedly tried cock sucking. This was something different, a pungence that reminded her of a hot torch of virility.

Susan let her tongue slip over the underside of his cock, and she discovered that she could actually feel the ridge-like veins of lust-heated blood that surged into his naked stiffness and made it throb and quiver with hard, anxious masculinity.

It was a thrilling sensation that she had been without for so long that she had nearly forgotten how it felt. The warm, enticing glow of her womanhood made her realize in the very pit of her soul that her handsome boss was feverish with passion for her. She had tried to convince herself that she didn't want him. But now that she had his prick in her mouth, she knew how much she really needed him. Susan looked at his hairy balls, swelling in manly magnificence. Reaching out, she gently touched them. This got him all the more aroused.

As long as Jennifer didn't know about this, it wouldn't matter, Susan reasoned. But she, too, was thinking of Jennifer and how much she wanted to be alone with her and eat her pussy.

At this moment, the big hard stud was insisting Susan take all of his inches. Instinctively, Susan's hands went up the insides of his firm, muscular thighs. Her fingers opened and then closed around the dangling orbs of his testicles, Heavy and bloated with hot cum.

Groaning hungrily, she pushed her face into the bushy thicket of John's pubic hair, her nostrils flaring with renewed desire. John held her closely. Little did he realize all of the office was watching on closed-circuit TV. If he had any idea they were observing him, his cock would have shrunk in an instant. But right now, it remains hard and throbbing with sexual desire.

"Hey, Susan, that's more like it. Open wide and let it slide down your throat. Hhhmmmm, baby... you're learning fast. Or maybe you know more than I thought."

Susan managed to tilt her head upward to look at him. He saw the smoky mist of feminine passion smoldering in her brown eyes. Leaning over, he let his hands slip down to her bosoms.

Finally, he unzipped her dress, lowering the metallic zipper down her smooth back and then slipping the dress from her shoulders one side at a time. She wiggled to help him, and he pushed her dress down to her waist, then reached around her narrow, unblemished back to unfasten her brassiere.

The snaps opened reluctantly, and the halves of her white lacy bra fell away and dropped down her arms to her elbows.

Her breasts fell free, and Susan could not stifle the gasp of delicious wickedness that surged from her throat even as it filled with her boss's cock. Her fingers slipped everywhere between his legs at once, lightly fondling the huge fleshy orbs of his balls, stroking the wispy hairs of his inner thighs. Even a daring caress that eased upward between the cheeks of his firm, sinewy buttocks brought him still greater pleasure. She found herself stroking him there, extending her delicate fingers into the tautly clenched fissure of his buttocks. John relaxed his ass cheeks, and her fingers probed, delicately exploring the firm, sinewy flesh of his buttocks, a single finger daring to cautiously poke at the nether ring of his anus.

Susan knew she would never have dared such a thing with anyone but John. She felt compelled to answer her wildest, long-suppressed urges tonight. She knew that she was a frantically erotic woman. Beneath the chic facade, she was a horny whore.

"Hhmmm, Susan... all right, all right!" he groaned appreciatively as her cheeks hollowed the thick, pulsing stiffness of his prick, and her tongue swirled wetly around it, sucking and licking, occasionally daring to tease him with a flick of her tongue tip at the tiny slit of its bulbous tip.

John leaned over her as she sucked and gulped ravenously at the turgid hardness of his erection, and he cupped one of her large voluptuous breasts in his palms and lifted it.

The erotic scene that the office employees were watching had an effect. The men were placing their arms around the girlfriends and squeezing their breasts. At the same time, the women were reaching down to grip their lover's crotches.

The girls could feel the hard penises under the material of the pants. Ziggy Falcon was standing near Jennifer now. He looked down at her as she looked up at him. His smoldering eyes registered pleasure as he saw her shapely bosoms. He put his arm around her, and she felt the tingle of desire racing up and down her spine in spite of the fact she was tormented by the erotic spectacle she was witnessing on the huge television screen in living color.

As John Williams plunged his prick into Susan Moore's mouth, fresh waves of arousal swept over him. He enjoyed the delicious sensation of her lips gripping his sliding prick. Her lips opened wider, and she managed to give voice to the sizzling pain of John's driving cock slicing down her throat.

"Don't worry," he grinned mockingly as he sent a deep punishing cock thrust down her throat.

It was one thing to look at Susan getting her throat fucked in the movies. It was quite another thing to be in the same position herself. And Susan choked, coughed, and nearly gagged, but all the while, John Williams pushed her face into his loins with his free hand and forced her to take every inch of his long, thick erection until finally she had to swallow or choke. His prick slithered wetly down her gullet, hotly lubricated with her own saliva.

"You see, baby, it's easy if you relax," he gasped as the taut muscles of her throat gave way and began to massage his naked stiffness like a milkmaid's fingers.

He moved around slightly and then eased himself onto the edge of the bed.

"There, that's better... I want to feel those nice hot tits of yours."

Both of John's hands reached for the jiggling warmth of her bare breasts. Susan's eyes closed tightly as a shameless groan of pleasure gushed from her throat when John's fingers began to earnestly caress her sensitive breasts, tweaking her crinkly pink nipples and squeezing the soft, heavy globes of her breasts until they throbbed with a dizzying mixture of pleasure and salacious pain.

At this point, he spread his hairy legs wide and pushed on the back of Susan's head until she was practically wedged between his muscular thighs. His cock was completely sheltered in the warm, wet grip of her lips and her tongue, and she was sucking it now with such fervent arousal that she grunted and moaned as her tongue slurped incitingly around the stiffened hunk of virile maleness.

Susan's cheeks hollowed, and her nostrils flared luridly as she tried to breathe and suck rapaciously on this delicious love muscle. His hands coarsely gripped at her jiggling naked breasts, fanning the already hot flames of desire in her long-emptied belly until it seemed that a blow torch had been held between her legs, and she could feel the sticky, warm wetness of her love juices damp and hot between her thighs.

All at once, John grabbed the back of Susan's head with both hands and slammed her nostrils into the bushy dampness of his pubic hair. John groaned, and his pelvis shuddered-and then a tidal wave of seething white cum gushed up from his heavily bloated balls and along the pipe-hard length of his cock until it burst free with a splattering ricochet of sticky heat that erupted down Susan's throat with the intensity of machine-gun fire.

"Susan, baby, don't stop sucking now," John grunted, his head back and his eyes closed tightly. "Get it all... all of it... every cock-sucking drop."

Susan nearly choked on the thick, creamy wetness that filled her mouth and gushed, swirling down the back of her throat in sticky waves. She managed to swallow it all down in gulp after gulp of hot, rich cum. Susan loved the taste of it, the thick cream-like texture, so warm and deliciously sweet with the pungent spice of virile maleness.

Now with all his heavy cum down her throat and his cock softly deflating in the taut caressing grip of her lips, she needed it more than ever... between her legs, where it counted.

Susan was burning alive from the inside out with insatiable, frantic cock hunger. John pulled his flaccid cock from her lips and held it with his hand, encircling her mouth with the sensitive purplish head, smearing her lips with the last traces of semen that oozed from the tiny glans.

"There's some more, Susan, lick it all now – now!" he commanded.

Susan did not hesitate but extended her tongue and swiped the sweet-tasting remnants of his orgasm from her quaking lips.

"You like that, baby?"

Susan nodded shamelessly, unable to look at John's face as she knelt between his legs like a cheap whore.

"Come on, did you like it?" John insisted, eager to degrade her some more.

"Yes, yes, damn it, I did," she admitted.

When she finally said she enjoyed this kind of sex with him, her girlfriend Jennifer, who was watching, felt hot tears scalding her cheeks. Ziggy, the rock star who was watching her closely, couldn't figure out why she was almost crying. Maybe, he calculated, she was hot for him and feared she might not go to bed with him. Ziggy could understand this, but he never could understand the true reason for the scalding tears that flowed freely down her cheeks.

Operating under the delusion of his own ego trip, Ziggy smiled at her and fondled her breasts momentarily.

"I'm not gonna leave you, baby," he whispered.

Jennifer looked up at him appreciatively. The sympathy that he was displaying was wrongly placed. Nevertheless, he was sympathetic and the rock star from London who had the audience at The Radio City Music Hall howling just a few short hours earlier.

Once more, Jennifer's eyes focused on the television screen as she saw the closed-circuit performance that John and Susan were giving the office force, unknown to them.

John Williams smiled down at Susan and laughed mockingly.

"You're hornier than ever now, right?"

She nodded.

"Well, Susan, I promised you a good time and always keep my word. Let's change places, but I want to get the rest of that dress off. And your panties, too. I'll bet they're probably stuck to your crotch."

Susan's cheeks reddened in humiliation, for she knew what

John said was true. He helped her get to her feet, her knees feeling like watery gelatin.

Tremblingly, Susan stood before John as he finished undressing her, easing her rumpled dress over her hips and pushing it down her bare legs to the floor.

Susan opened her eyes and saw a dozen mocking reflected images of herself in the room's mirrored walls. She closed her eyes tightly to hide from the accusing visions of her own nakedness. With the acquiescence of a slave, she allowed John to undress her. She was too much in need of what he had to offer much resistance.

"Good girl," John smiled eagerly. "You keep yourself in really nice shape."

Breathing huskily, John began to peel her lacy bikini panties over the flare of her womanly hips. Susan shivered as she felt his thumbs hook in the elastic of her panties and began to tug them downward like a flag of surrender. She was utterly and unquestionably his now, his love slave.

He noticed the wetness at the crotch of her lacy panties as he rolled them over her hips, exposing the sparse fleecy curls of her pubic vee and the wispy traces of hair that edged down the apex of her belly. He stretched the elastic outward and past the flare of her curvaceous hips, and now Susan's genitals were nakedly and unguardedly exposed, and through the downy softness of her pubic hair, he could see the thin, moisture-rimmed slit of her pussy. Tiny beaded drops of her own newly discovered excitement. She wanted to feel John's tongue deep between her thighs, his lips hotly caressing the naked pink folds of her sizzling genitals.

"Just lay back on the sofa," John grinned up from between her trim, supple thighs. "I'll do the rest. You'll never forget this night, and I won't either."

Jennifer watched and listened to the words John had just said. She realized she would never forget this awful night either. Yet she did feel somewhat protected by Ziggy, whose body was close to her now as his arms wrapped around her. She couldn't pull away from the erotic sight of sex on the big screen television.

5 – The Backdoor

Susan was stretching out on the sofa, her legs doubled back and the soles of her bare feet resting on the wall. Her knees were up, and her thighs were obscenely splayed as John's face pressed between them into the sizzling dampness of her pussy.

Hastily John pushed her thighs even farther open with the backs of his hands and nuzzled into the pungent warmth of her cunt. Susan groaned loudly as his tongue tip brushed again over the shuddering little marble of her clitoris, then swiped downward with a single thick stroke that took his tongue from the trembling bud of her clitoris, over the wet, warm fissure of her cunt, to the tautly puckered little hole of her anus.

"Ohhh," Susan gasped, and then her voice trailed off to a gurgling silence as her boss licked her again and again, fervent strokes of lust-stirring lasciviousness that made her shiver and tremble with erotic desire.

John spread her pussy lips with his thumbs, slipping his tongue and lips deeply into the steaming fissure of her pink, moist cunt.

Susan squirmed like she was in pain, but it was not hurt that made her groan and shudder so violently it was the gnawing anguish of her own ravenous sexual passions.

John licked her hotly, again and again, his tongue thick and through her ravaged mind's eye a foot long. Susan shook convulsively as her lover licked up and over the tiny nerve-filled node of her clitoris, and then his delicious laving narrowed to that super-sensitive little pearl. Susan began to climb the walls with groaning, gut-wrenching lusts.

"Lick my pussy, you beautiful man, ahhh, yes... lick it... make me cum!"

She was becoming more excited now as she groaned in near hysteria. The boss began to swipe his tongue up the narrow, moist fissure of her pussy with rapid, long licks that were turning her into a screaming bundle of overloaded nerves.

John held the lips of her pussy widely apart, slipping his tongue tip deeply into the clinging pinkness of her sizzling vagina. He could feel the walls of her cunt nibbling at his tongue, urging him deeper into the prolonged, hungry heat of her womanhood. Her pubic hair tickled his nose, and this excited him. He could sniff her delicious aroma.

Letting his tongue lick over the little bud of her clitoris brought it hard and alive now with sex-charged energy. John's tongue swirled around it... over it... and then his lips fastened onto the nerve-laden little pearl, his teeth gently nibbling it as Susan's groans of passion became louder, ever louder.

John reached up and around her hips for two soft, delicious handfuls of jiggling breasts, and Susan let loose another stirring moan of submission, grinding her hips down against his face and lips. There was no mistaking her orgasm when it began to come. First, she gasped loudly as if in pain, and then there was a long, dramatic pause as every muscle in her body seemed eager and tense-and then it came, with the strength of a dozen naked women!

"Ahhh, yesssss!" Susan hissed through clenched teeth.

Suddenly her entire body shuddered, convulsing with

orgasmic energy, and he felt his cheeks flooded with the gushing warmth of her pussy load. Susan shook and groaned repeatedly, each time louder than before... and then she was still. The only sound in John's inner office was the painful rasp of her labored breathing. And then the lascivious slurping noise of her pussy lips as his tongue swirled between them one last time. Susan was lying there with her eyes closed when she felt his hands on her tingling flesh. She looked at him through the slits of her passion-moist eyelids.

"Wow!" she exclaimed. "You sure know how to lick pussy."

As the office force looked at the television screen, they couldn't help but be reminded that they were looking at a sleazy porno movie. Only it was more stimulating, more arousing than any porno picture as it was for real. They would play it back some time for John and Susan. Certainly, it would give them a jolt of surprise. John had gone too far into the wild and forbidden world of adulterous sex to even care. But Susan was a young woman, and it would bother her to think everyone had seen her kneel before him, obeying him as he plunged his rigid prick into her mouth.

At this point, Ziggy Falcon motioned for Jennifer.

"Maybe we can find a place," he told her, "where nobody will see us. Do you see that couple over there?"

Jennifer looked into a darkened corner of the room. Sure enough, one guy was going down on his date. He had his head between her thighs. Even though her skirt was protectively over his head, it was obvious what was happening.

"I guess he likes to eat pussy," Ziggy grinned. "Slurp, slurp... delicious."

Jennifer was no longer suspicious of what the rock star from London had in mind for her. His hand patted her vagina.

"You shouldn't do that, Ziggy," Jennifer told him.

Jennifer couldn't help wondering if this was part of Susan's strategy. Even though Susan had acted as if she didn't want to have sex with John, she nevertheless had complied with his every request. All at once, Jennifer figured she might have been brought from North Carolina as a foil for Ziggy. A virgin offered up for a rock idol's sacrifice. Horrible thoughts like this spun through her mind as she realized Ziggy obviously had the hots for her.

"How did you like the concert tonight?" Ziggy insisted on knowing.

"It was very interesting," Jennifer assured him.

"That's what I thought," he smiled.

"Look what's happening on the screen now," Ziggy observed.

Sure enough, John was making more sexual demands upon his secretary, Susan Moore.

"Now," John told her, "why don't you kneel again? I like to see a woman on her knees looking up at me."

Susan could take it no longer. Once she had been satisfied, she didn't feel the pressuring need for orgasmic relief. With daring and conviction, she told John what she thought of him.

"Did anybody ever tell you you're a sex maniac, John?"

"All the time, baby," he replied. "And it's the nicest compliment anyone ever paid me."

Susan's eyes widened in amazement as she realized nothing she could say would bother him.

"It just isn't normal to do things like this," she told him.

"So what is normal?" John laughed. "So normal people have killed each other in World War I and World War II. Over fifty million people, I guess. Maybe that's normal. I don't go by what other people think or do, baby. I do what I enjoy."

Pleasure was John Williams' principle. And it was his pleasure to force Susan Moore to submit to every bizarre sexual desire that he ever felt surging through his loins.

"You're impossible, John," Susan shook her head and laughed as she realized he was without moral codes.

"But I'm exciting," John insisted, his eyes glistening with lustful desire as he reached out to fondle her bosoms.

Gripping the crinkly nipples of her breast buds, he squeezed them.

"Stop it, you're hurting me," she insisted.

"Feels good to me," John smiled as he reached out and let his hand cup her buttocks.

Squeezing her ass cheeks, he sent shivers of tingling delight racing up and down her spine with a new-found sexual electricity.

"Lay off, John," she told him. "We shouldn't be doing things like this."

John was paying little attention to her now. He was bound and determined that he would do as he wanted.

"Sweetheart," he told her, "did you ever try a hot-and-cold cock suck?"

Susan didn't know what he was talking about.

Watching the action on the giant television screen, Jennifer Davis felt nervous and tense. Ziggy Falcon held her tightly, and her eyes focused on the television screen. She could see that John was determined to have more sex with Susan Moore. He forced Susan to reach again for his prick and pull it until it was hard again. Then, grinning, he told her to bend over the sofa.

"What do you want to do?" Susan blurted nervously.

"Shut up," John snapped, and then he grinned. "I'm gonna fuck your cute asshole."

Shaking her head, she begged him not to.

"Relax," he told her, "you'll like it when you get used to it."

John was stroking his heavy prick as Susan bent over the sofa. Everyone from the office force-watched and listened in utter horror. There was nothing Susan Moore could do. Absolutely nothing. It was obvious John intended to defile her in every way possible. Yet not one person in the entire office crew dared defy John.

"Yes, baby," he assured her, "you'll love it when I shove it right up there."

John was crawling behind her now. And he placed his hands on her back, pressing her forward. Then she felt his heavy penis insinuating itself in the crease of her buttocks as he slowly eased forward.

"Soft as velvet," John said as he eased his prick right up her ass crack.

Reaching forward, he clutched at her breasts, kneading harshly, twisting one nipple into rock hardness between his fingers.

"You've sure got tits," he told her as he brutally began fingering her nipple.

At the same time, he was plunging his prick in her ass. Susan Moore felt her stomach chum wildly. John had spread her buttocks apart, and he began to taunt her tightly puckered anus without mercy.

"Stop it," she begged. "Please, don't."

John was paying no attention to her pleading cries. He was enjoying the fact that she was so tight.

"Your ass is as tight as a drum," he told her. "Just made for old John."

At this point, he was so excited he was trembling. When he didn't instantly shove his prick right up her asshole, a couple of men from the office force who were watching on the closed-circuit television gasped, "Fuck her ass, John. Get your cock right up there."

Susan's quivering buttocks indicated how fearful she was. John's hot hands opened her soft, quaking ass cheeks, drawing her buttocks apart even further, only making Susan squirm in more agony. She tried to hold them together by tensing the smooth ivory spheres, but it was useless. Susan felt obscenely naked beneath John's lust-filled eyes as he pressured her ass cheeks open. She could feel the cool air on the hot, perspiring inner sides.

Tears suddenly wet her cheeks as he drove steadily forward. Reaching underneath, John's finger probed at her pussy. At the same time, the sharp pain of his cock worming into her asshole drove her out of her mind. Automatically, her muscle reaction tried closing her buttocks, and she gripped his prick in her nether hole before he could ram it in all the way.

"Look at your asshole work," he smiled. "Baby, cooperate

with me. Don't tense up. Relax so I can slip it in easily. Otherwise, I'll shove it up, and it'll hurt like the devil."

It taunted and tortured her so much that she felt she might as well give in to him. The degrading act of being sodomized was the last straw as far as Susan Moore was concerned. Sure, she liked working for John Williams and had a good position as his private secretary. However, to be forced to lie down like this and accept his prick up her ass was something she hadn't counted on.

"Now I'm gonna give you a real hot fuck," he told her. "Come on, Susan, fuck back."

Once more, he thrust his thick prick deeper into the tight, rubbery channel of her asshole. She grunted painfully from deep in her chest while he rutted and sawed in and out of her helplessly exposed, unresisting anus, lewdly stretching the warm, velvety passage in preparation for the entry that was to follow.

In complete despair, Susan relaxed in resigned surrender. She lay pressed almost completely on her stomach on the sofa's edge. John's legs wedged between hers, forcing her ass cheeks up. And then she felt his naked loins as he pumped forward.

"I'm gonna give you a wild ass fuck," he promised her as he aimed the head of his prick directly at her crinkled little anus.

The agony of having him stretch her asshole with his thrusting cock had her shaking. Once more, John spread her buttocks wide open with his thumbs, then rode further onto her to slowly draw the huge head of his cock up through her butt. She jerked at the soft contact.

"Get it over with, damn it," she exclaimed, as she felt the entire full length of his shaft driving in the soft-spread crevice of her ass, its tip poised at her snug, throbbing anus.

She froze in terror as she felt him levering himself on his elbows so he could move his hips forward, guiding the knob of his rigid member directly at the flexing little hole of her back passage.

Susan felt John's rough hands running over her back, neck, and shoulders, then beneath her to maul her breasts brutally. Then Susan felt John's prick as it pushed painfully against her anus, and she gaped wild-eyed as the brutally stiffened shaft suddenly shoved her tightly resisting sphincter with splitting pain, and she knew sheer horror as she'd never known before. His cock was stretching the tiny orifice obscenely to grip over like a glove and absorb the probing tip of his huge penis. Pain spread through her like a raging fire, and she looked over her shoulder to see the grin of triumph on his face. He thrust his hips heavily forward, burrowing half of the fleshy, turgid staff into the soft, velvety passage of her hairless rectum.

"Fuck," he exclaimed as he rammed it to her, and her buttocks mechanically jerked and twisted beneath the depraved assault.

Her every move only served to impale her deeper, for with each buck and lurch of her tortured body, John's massive prick was skewering that much further into her desperately resisting rectal orifice.

"Fuck, baby, fuck," he snapped as he went on pumping her.

He was riding up her ass with deep, penetrating stabs now. She hated it but was completely helpless to resist.

"Beautiful," he exclaimed as he forced her buttocks open in the air, his knees moving in between her thighs to push them wide apart, spreading her ass cheeks even more to help his prick enter in and sodomize her.

Susan felt hot tears coming from her eyes as the pain spread and made her stomach convulse with the sickness that rose to her throat. However, the office force that was watching the developing sodomy scene enjoyed it. The girls were slipping the guys' cocks out and pulling on them obscenely. Relentlessly now, John was pumping his prick up her asshole, enjoying it enormously.

"Oh, baby, you're tight all right," he told her. "You haven't been all screwed out till you're loose. That's the kind of fuck I like."

He pumped all the way up her ass to the very depths. The pain went on, and each thrust brought muffled grunts from deep in her throat.

"Baby, let me get it all in," he panted as he pummeled into her with longer, smoother strokes, shoving the entire length of his cock right up her rectum until she could feel his bloated balls slapping each time against her tightly spread buttocks.

The depraved union had stimulated all of the people of the office force who watched the closed-circuit television.

"I'd like to fuck your asshole," one young office worker observed as the girl beside him pulled on his throbbing, long penis and bent over to lick it.

"Not in your life," the girl smiled who was watching.

All the time this was happening, the London rock star Ziggy Falcon was getting friendlier with Jennifer. Jennifer couldn't help but respond. He was so handsome and so hot for young Jennifer.

John Williams' massive, throbbing cock was driving into the very depths of Susan's bowels now. The young, naked, brunette secretary was helplessly impaled.

"Now I'm getting it," he told her. "Baby, doesn't it feel good?"

Susan couldn't answer. Finally, she gasped as he kept ramming it in.

"Take it easy, John," she begged.

She felt his balls smack tightly against the spread cheeks of her buttocks as he drove in. Susan whimpered loudly, both in the agony and the pain of the debased shame of the act. She hated what was happening. He was driving it in without mercy now. With massive, angry cock thrusts slicing deep into her soft, tender body, she wondered how much of this she could stand. At the same instant, she felt his fingers slipping along her moist pussy and crazily plunging into her cunt.

"In and out, baby," he told her as he went on driving in her tight asshole.

With mean, hard strokes, he was developing a rhythmic cadence.

"If I had another guy fucking on the other side," he told her, "you'd get a double thrill.

You'd like to get it both ways."

Susan was outraged at the thought of such a thing. Apparently, it wasn't enough to be sodomized. John was contemplating having another man ramming his prick into her cunt. She could imagine him tearing her.

"Ahhh, I'm almost there," John gasped as he pulled his glistening, thick prick from her tightly stretched asshole.

Pistoning his prick into her now with lust-glazed eyes, he looked at her excitedly.

"You sure have a beautiful ass," he told her. "Now, if you would just cooperate with me, you'd get it off."

He watched as his prick disappeared in her asshole and then slid out. Her ass seemed to suck down on his cock, tugging him tighter into her behind.

"Ohhh, ram it to you, baby," he told her as he jabbed hard up her ass.

Shamed and aching, her head tossing back and forth, she begged for him to stop.

"That's enough," she told him. "You're hurting me.

Ziggy whispered to Jennifer Davis as her eyes still remained glued on the TV set, "He is a bit cruel."

Once more, John's huge cock rammed up Susan's ravaged ass. It was useless for her to complain, for he was determined to fuck her until he got his rocks off.

"Ohhh, stop it," Susan begged as she felt him ramming in, debasing her beyond all reason.

He'd ravaged her body, and she wished that he would end this sadistic sex play.

"Grind your hips," he told her.

She began to undulate her buttocks and squeeze with her anal muscles on his hard thick shaft as it bored into her with such fierce force. And then she found herself suddenly enjoying it. It was amazing what was happening. With each obscenely vicious thrust, she found herself liking it.

"I told you, you'd get to like it," he said as he kept pounding the blood-filled head of his prick up her defenseless rectum.

His ramming man meat had started to excite her. Sudden waves of erotic sensation saturated her entire being. Nothing registered any longer but the magnificent cock fucking her rhythmically, insanely. She rocked back and forth as he continued stabbing her asshole.

"I'm almost there," he told her. "Just keep pumping it."

John went on driving in like a wild man. Now, he was desperately eager to have her say she enjoyed it.

"Do you like it?" he asked.

"Ohhh, ahhh, yes, yes," Susan replied in a soft voice as he went on plunging up her rectal passage.

Faster and faster, he was fucking her now, and with every stab, she gave herself up to wilder sexual abandonment.

"I want it," Susan cried out. "Fuck me, John. I want every inch of your prick in my asshole."

It was wonderful now, the mounting exotic bliss of his stabbing, slippery prick driving up her ass. Her brain reeled-nothing mattered but the tremendous sensations of erotic rapture about to burst inside of her asshole.

"Now, now," she begged, "fill me. Let me feel you coming. I want it."

As his hot liquid sperm shot deep into her asshole, her own orgasm seized her, sending delicious spasms of sensations rocketing through her, and she could feel every contraction of his huge cock as it jerked out its load of hot, white cream, deep up into her contracting bowels. John gasped and grunted as he rutted up her ass. He was breathing heavily now as his jerking prick continued spewing its thick, hot jets of semen deep into her quivering body.

"Ohhh, fuck, fuck," he exclaimed as he finished screwing her.

Easing his slippery cock from her tight asshole, he gently patted her buttocks.

"You're a good girl," he told her.

Gently massaging her own bare bottom and shaking her head, Susan Moore declared, "A girl can get killed when you fuck her like that."

That brought a round of laughter to everyone who was seated in the office and watching their sexual performance on the closed-circuit television screen. Ziggy grinned at Jennifer.

"You've got a cute ass, honey," he told her. "I sure would like to teach you what I know about sodomy."

6 – Alone with a Rock Star

It frightened Jennifer Davis to hear the London rock star talking to her about sodomy. But what was even more frightening were the lusty desires that she felt deep within herself. Ziggy Falcon was so handsome that she wanted him, yet she knew it wasn't right.

"How about you and me going up to the penthouse suite?" he asked her.

"No, no... I couldn't," Jennifer insisted.

"Sure you could," he told her. "You could do anything you want."

Jennifer slowly raised her eyes to his. She looked at him with dual emotions. Somehow, she wanted him, yet she didn't. He looked at her and told her, "I hope you find me appealing."

"Of course I do," she gasped. "You're very handsome, Ziggy, and tonight, you really proved to me what a fantastic entertainer you are."

"Well, get smart," he whispered, "and show me that you can come alive. Why don't we go to that lovely penthouse with the perfect view now? You can see everywhere, John told me."

Why not? Jennifer was starting to think to herself. After all, Susan Moore had gotten into the predicament that she was in because she wanted to. John Williams had the hots for her, and she was anxious to play with his prick. It didn't take much convincing for Susan to go down on John and suck his cock off. However, it was not easy for her to give in to Ziggy's pleas.

"Do you live in Manhattan?" the rock star from London asked the new graduate of the women's college.

Shaking her head, Jennifer Davis told him she had just flown in from North Carolina.

"Let's go upstairs and talk some more," he insisted.

At this point, John and Susan weren't having sex anymore. They were drinking. Susan, apparently wanting to forget the awful things that she'd been forced to endure, was trying to cloud her brain with booze. Jennifer felt as though she'd been betrayed by Susan, who had let everyone in the office know what a slut she could be. Wanting to cling to something, Jennifer found herself pressing next to Ziggy.

"I think it's time we left, baby," he whispered softly in her right ear, playfully pushing her beautiful blond hair to one side.

Turning away from the television screen and not paying any attention to the wild action that was going on in the room, Jennifer and Ziggy stepped out into the hall and took the elevator up to the penthouse suite.

"There's a double bolt lock on the door, John told me," Ziggy smiled, "so we won't have to worry about anybody coming up here."

What John Williams had yet to reveal to Ziggy Falcon, however, was the fact that the Empire Vinyl Records penthouse suite was also on a closed-circuit television setup.

"What a fantastic place this is," Jennifer exclaimed as Ziggy opened the double doors to the penthouse suite.

All of the lights of Manhattan were spread out below and twinkling like diamonds, rubies, emeralds, and sapphires.

"I've always wanted to see Manhattan," Ziggy exclaimed, "but I never thought I would have such a nice welcoming committee."

The twisted expression of lust that contorted his half-smirking countenance suddenly bothered young Jennifer Davis.

"But you didn't get me up here to look at the lights of Manhattan, did you?" she asked.

Ziggy's lust-filled eyes told her the raw, naked truth.

"Why don't we just sit here and talk awhile?" he asked. "Then how about something to smoke?"

The young girl shook her head. She was cringing at the thought of smoking grass.

"You saw them downstairs," he reminded her. "Everybody smokes grass."

A look of amazement came over Jennifer's face as she realized how natural it was as far as Ziggy Falcon and the rock record crowd were concerned to smoke grass.

"Go ahead, you'll relax," he told her with a soft, lulling voice as he handed her the cigarette and lit up his own.

"All right," she finally agreed.

As the two of them sat on a brown leather sofa overlooking the lights of the city, Ziggy began feeling her tender bosoms, tweaking and pinching at the tiny pink nipples through the sultry fabric of her dress until they burst into painful hardness.

"What are you trying to do?" she asked him.

"I want you to enjoy yourself," he said, as his eyes locked

greedily onto the sensuous sight of her upthrusting bosoms, each curvaceous line visible through the clinging Quiana fabric of her pink dress.

How Jennifer wished that she hadn't listened to Susan. But she'd taken her advice and had gone braless this evening, so desperately wanting to make the right impression on this modern crowd in the rock record industry.

Ziggy slowly untied the front of Jennifer's dress, causing the fabric to fall caressingly to both sides of her ravishingly firm, rounded breast flesh. His eyes riveted magnetically onto the sensuous sight of her tantalizing orbs of sensuous tit flesh. He was pleased she wasn't wearing a brassiere, and the glow in his eyes gave her ample evidence that he was turning on. The titillating sight of her sensuous naked bosoms with their blood-red nipples stimulated him to new heights of sexual arousal.

"It's a pity," he told her, "that we can't perform naked on stage. That would really make it exciting."

Jennifer didn't know what to say to that.

"I would enjoy seeing you naked on stage," he smiled at Jennifer.

"Why, Ziggy," she gasped, "what a wicked thought."

Ziggy smiled and then let his hands gently caress her thighs.

"Why don't you reach over here and feel me?" the rock star smiled, realizing he had to take it slowly with her.

The expression on her face was gradually changing to one of desire instead of disgust.

"I'm all revved up," he told her. "You can feel it."

Taking Jennifer's hand, the London rock star placed it on his cock. It was obvious that he was ready to totally surrender to her. It did stimulate Jennifer to think that she was alone with this man, a man who other women worshiped. A sense of curiosity did whirl through her mind now as to what his prick would look like if she could see it naked.

"Don't you want to look at my filthy prick?" Ziggy Falcon grinned.

What he was doing now was unbelievable. He had the traits of a flasher as he slowly unzipped his fly. Jennifer couldn't bring herself to resist. A strange compulsion overtook her to do his bidding. She made another attempt at admonishing him.

"Ziggy, you shouldn't do that," she told him, completely at a loss to stop him.

Now that he had lost control, he paid no attention to her pleas. He was anxious to have her look at his throbbing manhood and determined to get her response. Pulling out his hard prick, he smiled proudly.

"This is what I've got," he told her, "and I want you to look at it."

With a sidelong glance, she saw his huge, throbbing shaft. All at once, she felt like a helpless prisoner. She knew that she wanted him, and if he forced her, she couldn't resist him. Ziggy was delighted with Jennifer Davis' responses. He was tired of hopelessly debauched women who would do anything at his bidding. And it pleased him that Jennifer was innocent and reticent about proceeding any further.

"I want to give you a good time," he told her, "but I can't unless you cooperate."

At this point, he reached for her hand and shamelessly placed it on his aroused thick penis flesh.

"I... I don't want to be forced to do anything," she said as the shame and degradation of what he was expecting suddenly surfaced in her mind.

However, Ziggy's charm and charisma were blotting out any thoughts of anything evil from her mind.

"Go ahead and pull on it," he told her as he gripped her hand around his throbbing man meat and pulled up and down.

There was an insane delight that seemed to spread across his face as he forced her to slowly jerk on the hot length of his pulsating manhood.

"Oh, I shouldn't be doing this," Jennifer argued, but with less determination than before.

Even though Jennifer Davis realized that what she was doing at this instant was the opposite of everything she had been taught, it didn't bother her. She was enjoying herself much too much to stop.

7 – Rock Hard

Once John Williams had finished getting his rocks off with Susan Moore, they both got dressed.

"Maybe I can work out a little bonus for you," John told her.

In the office where everyone was watching, an audible gasp of disgust arose in the room. It was apparent to everyone that John Williams was hiring girls based on screws, and this was getting everyone angry.

"Why thank you, John," Susan smiled.

Realizing they probably would be coming out of the office soon and not wanting them to learn they had been seen on closed-circuit television, one of the producers went swiftly to the corner of the room where he flicked off the switch for the television in John Williams' private office. However, he was amazed when he saw what was on the television screen. He had inadvertently turned on the closed-circuit television in the penthouse suite on top of the building.

Jennifer Davis and the London rock star Ziggy Falcon sat beside each other on a sofa. Everyone howled with laughter. As John and Susan came out to see what all the laughter was about, they both were shocked and stunned to see what was happening on closed-circuit television.

"What a performance," John laughed good-naturedly. "Let's see how he makes out with this nice girl."

Susan Moore was outraged by the sight she saw. There

was her beautiful, shapely, blonde roommate girlfriend. It was obvious Jennifer Davis was giving in to the charismatic appeal of Ziggy Falcon, the London rock star. It really got her furious. She wanted to go right up there and make a fuss about it.

Evil, dark thoughts surfaced in Susan Moore's mind. She had a pearl-handled pistol that she'd placed on her desk in another room. Susan told John that she had to get something.

"I've got grass for you, honey," he said as he opened up a package of cigarettes that he had used to cover up the fact he really had some weed.

"Oh, John, I didn't mean that," she told him.

"It's something else I left on my desk."

Susan Moore went into her private office. She rummaged around for a moment in the drawer on the right-hand side and finally picked up the pearl-handled pistol. She didn't turn on any lights, for she didn't want anyone to see if they should happen to stumble into her office. But the desire swept through her to kill John Williams. And then she came to her senses.

That wouldn't be fair. After all, she and John had carried on in a wild round of sex. Jennifer was only human, and it had been a year since they had last been together. Perhaps Jennifer had carried on with men during her absence. That would be perfectly natural, she reasoned. Yet she was torn two ways. Even though it would be natural for Jennifer to finally find a man she could relate to, she did feel a tinge of jealousy and decided perhaps a pistol would be the only way to end it for all of them.

Life in Manhattan had been difficult for Susan, and

sometimes, she felt as though she would like to jump off the top of a building. She knew one man who had done this, and she envied him. But she didn't have the guts for it. Slipping the pearl-handled pistol into her purse, Susan closed the desk drawer and quietly went back to the office party.

The waiters were serving more champagne, and she needed some. She would have to be stoned out of her mind to watch what happened between the rock star and her female lover.

When she returned, she was surprised to see Ziggy Falcon had pulled his pants down and was trying to guide Jennifer Davis over his throbbing male member. Everyone who was watching except Susan was laughing. John noticed this and was disturbed.

"Now, don't be a killjoy," he told her. "That's really fantastic entertainment. I knew we were gonna watch his show... but I had no idea he would perform like this!"

Jennifer, who was pulling on the London rock idol's pulsating penis, felt herself becoming hotter for his cock. She was curious to know what the sensation of slipping her mouth over his penis would be like.

"Why don't you go down there?" the rock idol suggested.

"I've never done it before," Jennifer said rather shyly.

That brought a round of laughter from everyone in the office.

"That girl must have just gotten out of college," one person shouted.

Susan Moore was so angry at that point she felt like pulling out the pearl-handled pistol and shooting the man who'd made the obscene remark. However, she restrained herself and once more followed a waiter who was carrying a silver tray of champagne glasses around the room. She stopped him and reached out for a glass.

"This is delicious," she enthused. "Thank you so much."

Returning to where she was seated next to John Williams, Susan looked at the television screen once more. It was all she could do to keep smiling and control her honest responses. She knew John would hate her if she ever revealed what she truly felt.

At this point, Ziggy suggested that he take off his clothes.

"Why?" Jennifer insisted.

"Because," he explained, "it makes it easier for what I have in mind."

Many of the people in the office who were listening to this comment laughed. Seconds later, the famous rock idol Ziggy Falcon was stripping for them all. That made the office crowd howl with laughter. However, when they caught sight of his huge, throbbing cock they realized it was no laughing matter.

Little Jennifer Davis, the beautiful blonde from the East Coast, was learning about sex sooner than she no doubt had expected.

"Now," Ziggy Falcon told Jennifer, "I'll just take off my shirt and then my pants."

Tossing his shirt aside, the rock idol pulled off his shoes and socks and then removed his pants and shorts. He stood before her, completely naked. Some of the girls who were watching the closed-circuit television screen whistled and applauded raucously.

"Wow!" one secretary who was chewing gum grinned as she looked at her boyfriend. "He's well hung," she observed.

"Get back here to jerking my cock," her boyfriend insisted as he got angry over the fact his girl was watching the rock idol standing there naked on the TV screen instead of paying attention to his erotic needs.

Recognizing Jennifer was not going to undress unless he helped her, Ziggy Falcon stepped naked over to the beautiful blonde girl. She lowered her eyes as if she couldn't look up at him. He drew her dress down over her shoulders with a slow, seductive movement until it fell in gentle caressing folds around her waist. The elasticized waistline held the dress firmly in place below her full, ripe, lush breasts, which jutted forth in all their tantalizing splendor.

Ziggy's fingertips reached out to pinch her crinkly, fleshed, dark nipples until they were blood-red and tingling with lusty excitement.

Next, Ziggy's determined fingers went to work removing her dress entirely. He tugged forcefully at the elasticized waist of her alluring pink Quiana dress, pulling the lustrous fabric downward further and further until it lay in cascading folds at her trim ankles.

Ziggy caught his breath as he got his first look at her ravishing body, nude from the waist up and clad in lacy black bikini panties and a flimsy black garter belt holding up her sheer nylon stockings from the waist down. What a fantastic sight she made in her obvious shyness as she revealed herself to the handsome London rock star with the smoldering, dark, passionate eyes that seemed to devour her very being. His lust-incited passions were raging close to the boiling point as his hands trembled slightly when he removed the dress from about her ankles and tossed it carelessly aside, the soft fabric billowing gracefully as it gently drifted to the floor.

Reaching down, Ziggy felt Jennifer's crotch. She was wet there, and he knew what she needed.

"You're a beautiful girl," he told her, "and you ought to be fed a good-tasting cock every now and then. That's what you need."

He was smiling down at her as if he could eat her alive, and it wasn't going to be much longer before the monstrous hard-on he had was sliding into her mouth.

Stretching Jennifer out on the brown leather sofa in the magnificently furnished penthouse suite, Ziggy knew Jennifer was at a loss to resist his determined efforts. His eager fingers went to work again, quickly taking off her ivory-colored leather high-heeled sandals. Ziggy's eyes glowed with intense desire as he gazed at Jennifer's appealing body. It neared a state of complete nakedness as he expertly undressed her. He inhaled the aroma of her womanly scent combined with the enticing perfume she wore, a fragrance that flared in his nostrils excitedly.

Deftly, with a quick flick of his wrist, Ziggy removed Jennifer's black lacy garter belt, casually dropping it to the plush white carpet of the penthouse suite. His expert fingertips entwined themselves in the lacy fabric of her sheer black panties, pulling them down over her lush buttocks and sliding them provocatively down her thighs, lower and lower, until they, too, were discarded with practiced ease. Her sheer tan nylon stockings were rapidly drawn down her beautifully tapered thighs as Ziggy Falcon brought the shivering, trembling college graduate to total nudity.

Ziggy suggested that Jennifer should kneel, bend over and lick his prick and suck his balls.

"I could never do that," Jennifer insisted, looking up at him innocently with her radiant blue eyes.

There was something about the innocence of this young girl and breaking her in that really made Ziggy Falcon's body vibrate with erotic expectations.

"Reach for my prick," he told her. "Go ahead. Pull on my prick with one hand and massage my balls with the other."

Reaching out, Jennifer grasped Ziggy's manhood firmly. Pulling it slowly, she began getting him so excited he could hardly stand it. With warm, sensuous strokes on his cock meat, she got him so excited he was moaning and closing his eyes.

"Come on," he told her, "that's the way. Jack it, jack it."

With delicate strokes, she pulled on his throbbing manhood. And at the same time, she let her fingers gently slide across his balls.

"Keep that up," Ziggy urged Jennifer. "That's what I like."

The thing that would really excite him was if he could get her to bend over and slip her tongue over his cock and finally let him plunge it into her mouth.

"How would you like to taste me?" he winked at her.

Jennifer didn't reply. But Ziggy reached out and gripped her head. Gently, he edged her toward his huge erection.

"Just touch it with the tip of your tongue," he insisted.

Finally, reluctantly, Jennifer let her moist pink tongue tip slide in circles over the head of his pulsing, blood-engorged rod. And then she swept the entire length and width of his shaft with warm, sensuous strokes of her slicing tongue. Ziggy was enjoying this enormously. He could hardly wait for her to suck all of his prick in her mouth and slide up and down it.

"Eat it," he told her anxiously. "Suck it. Go down on me."

Her head bobbed up and down on his throbbing manhood. He was so excited now that his balls were trembling in raw, lustful arousal.

"Play with my ass," he told her.

Letting her hand fall from his balls, Jennifer gently massaged and caressed the rock idol's bare buttocks.

"A lot of women would like to be where you are, Jennifer," he told her, "so you do me the honor of giving me a good cock suck and an ass suck, and I'd really appreciate it."

This was the first time Jennifer had ever heard of such a thing.

"I... I don't believe I heard you right," she told him.

"Yes, I'm gonna give you the honor," he smiled again.

Placing his hands behind his head, he watched as she pulled on his meaty penis shaft.

"You said you were gonna give me the honor of licking your ass. I... don't believe I could do that. I've never done anything like that."

Jennifer was now hesitating and trying not to say anything that would anger Ziggy. It was obvious the rock idol had plenty of ego. Even though she was certain some women would stoop to anything, she knew that she would never perform such a degrading and debasing act as was being suggested of her at this moment.

"I said I wanted you to rim my asshole," he said firmly, as if amazed she couldn't appreciate the offer that he was making so generously.

"I've... I've never done anything like that," Jennifer said nervously, "and I've never heard of anything like that either."

It was quite apparent to Ziggy Falcon that she was bound and determined to beg off. But he was just as determined that she was going to do his sexual bidding.

"You'll love it once you get used to it," he smiled. "Just get your face down there and start licking gently around my buttocks. You'll get used to it. You'll like it if you'll only try it. Go ahead." It was next to impossible for Jennifer to stoop to such a degrading, debasing act, no matter how much he begged her. Yet as she felt the persuasiveness of his hand forcing her head down around his ass cheeks, she recognized that he meant business. Her tongue gently caressed his round, sinewy buttocks.

"Lick my ass," he begged, "lick it real nice. That's what I want, Jennifer, lick it."

Jennifer did not like the idea of doing what she was called upon to do. When the office force watched intently at what was happening on the closed-circuit television screen, they could hardly believe their eyes. The London rock star had angled his legs up in the air and was pulling them back. He was making no bones about what he expected the young girl to do for him.

As he held his knees and angled his ass to make it

convenient for her to lick his asshole, he told her she could pull on his prick while she ate out his ass.

"I really prefer this kind of sex," he told her. "I like to have a girl giving me a good rim job with her tongue."

Her mouth was caressing his bare, sinewy buttocks. But she still couldn't bring herself to let her tongue slide around his tight anus.

"Just put your hands on my ass and hold me," he told her, "and then lick quick."

The rock idol Ziggy Falcon was grinning with lusty desire as he felt Jennifer's tongue sliding around his ass crack. He put his hands behind his head and watched carefully as she sucked.

Finally, she pulled away and told him nervously, "You're asking me to do something perverted, Ziggy."

Ziggy burst out laughing.

"Perverted, my asshole," he smiled as he insisted she get down there and lick him some more.

She gripped his manly, firm buttocks and gently let her tongue tease around his ass crack. But that wasn't enough for him.

"I simply love getting my ass sucked," he explained, "and a lot of my female fans enjoy sucking on my but. You'll love it if you get your face in there and start licking. I want you to tongue fuck my asshole good."

He parted his buttocks for her, and then she rolled down on his behind. There was such burning intensity in the way that he requested her to rim him that she felt obligated. Gripping his bare ass cheeks, Jennifer let her tongue gently caress all around his ass crack. Yet she couldn't bring herself to stab her tongue right up his rectum as he had directed her to do.

"Why don't you do what I tell you to do?" the hot young rock star begged the beautiful blonde girl.

"I... I can't," she complained. "I can't suck your ass out."

He laughed as he heard her mouth the words. Jennifer was such an innocent, sweet-looking girl that it gave him a certain kind of warped pleasure to hear her say these obscene words.

"I'll bet you'd make a great ass licker," he assured her. "You won't know until you've tried it. Come on, do it for me. Rim me."

Ziggy smiled down at her and convinced her that she should at least try. Finally, she found her tongue sliding across his bare bottom. He reached down to pry his ass cheeks apart for her to make it easy. Suddenly, with a stiffening plunge, she ran her tongue right up his rectum.

"Oh, yes," he cried anxiously, "tongue fuck my asshole. I love it."

She grasped his buttocks firmly. Jennifer kept her tongue propelling right up his ass crack all the way.

"Now you're sucking," he gasped excitedly. "Ohhh, Jennifer, baby, lick my ass. Suck my butt!" Jennifer kept her eyes closed while she drilled her tongue right up his rectum.

In the meantime, Susan Moore was trembling with rage and indignation. She wanted to march right up to the penthouse and tell Ziggy Falcon to go to London and then to hell. However, John Williams restrained her.

"Say, that's a real nice girl you brought out here," he smiled. "I'll have to go to bed with her, too."

Laughing and pretending it didn't matter, Susan assured him that Jennifer would probably enjoy having sex with him.

"Maybe she can lick my asshole like she's doing it for him," John grinned suggestively.

Susan knew how to keep her feelings to herself, but it wasn't easy at this point. She was disgusted as she saw what was happening on the closed-circuit television screen. Her eyes riveted on what was taking place in the penthouse with the London rock star.

"Eat my ass out," Ziggy begged passionately.

In a blinding frenzy of erotic lust, Jennifer did as he begged her to. Her tongue surged up his asshole, stimulating him and arousing him every moment.

"Ohhh, baby," he exclaimed passionately, "now you're doing it. Reach for my prick. Jack my cock while you lick my butt."

Reaching up, Jennifer grasped Ziggy's firm, long manhood. She began pulling on his cock with heated fervor. She kept her tongue plunging right up his rectum at the same tempo as her hand jacked on his manhood.

"Ohhh, suck it, suck my ass out," he begged her frantically. "Lick it. Now you're doing it, just like that. Ohhh, keep your hand moving, too, honey. That's beautiful."

Jennifer was cooperating with Ziggy to give him the kind of erotic action that was driving him out of his mind with a sexual frenzy.

"Get your mouth over my prick," he begged her. "Suck me real quick. I want it."

Finally, she licked the head of his shaft. She capped his

cock with her mouth. Sucking down hungrily, he was pleased with her marvelous exhibition. She did have a wonderful way of entertaining him.

"Suck me," he begged frantically. "Suck my asshole."

The delicious thrills that he knew now had him flipping out. And Jennifer found now that she enjoyed having Ziggy's thick cock pumping relentlessly into her mouth. She groaned heavily around the thrusting thickness of his penis in humiliation and debasement of the acutest kind. Yet Jennifer continued to suck on him, increasing her efforts to give him pleasure without really understanding why. In masochistic abandon, she began to rock her open loins up and down as he pumped.

"Come on, baby," he told her, "fasten your lips on my prick. I want to flood your face with my cum."

She kept sucking on his thick manhood. Jennifer enjoyed opening her eyes and seeing his saliva-slick prick pumping in and out at a rapid-fire tempo.

"Yes," he hissed through clenched teeth as he gripped her head and kept ramming it to her.

His thicket of curly pubic hair tickled Jennifer's nose as she sucked up and down on his reckless, throbbing penis.

"Some fans tell me I taste real sweet," he told her as he quickened the tempo of his cruel thrusts.

Jennifer gripped Ziggy's hips and held him back so he wouldn't choke her with his powerful cock stabs. Ziggy enjoyed the feeling of her hands grasping his firm, rigid buttocks. She went on steadily licking at his juicy joint of male flesh.

"Ohhh, I like that," Ziggy gasped. "It's beautiful."

Jennifer's mouth moved up and down the length of his shaft. She reached down and massaged his balls.

"Now you're doing it," he told her. "Suck it, suck it."

She continued giving him the action he so desperately sought.

"I'm gonna shoot you," he gasped excitedly. "Just keep sucking. Don't stop."

The young rock star pumped into her mouth like a sex maniac. Jennifer enjoyed the feel of his ass cheeks and the flexing muscles.

"I like your hands all over me. Come on, baby, finger my asshole."

Parting his bare buttocks, she let her finger gently ease into his tight anus. It excited Ziggy to feel her finger slipping up his rectum. Now he was ramming it so hard he was slipping down her throat. She could feel the head of his shaft touching the back of her throat.

"Oh, baby, this is really fucking," he told her, his balls bouncing on her chin as he rammed it into her.

Jennifer felt totally purged of inhibitions now. She was cleansed of any depraved guilt feelings. The thrill of anticipation goaded her on. She was eager to feel his throbbing cock exploding. She wanted to taste him. Gripping his huge cock lewdly at its base, she slowly pulled on it. Jennifer could feel her own raging genital heat as his lust-bloated balls slapped against her hand as she pumped back and forth.

"Suck it," he told her. "Suck off!"

Jennifer kept her mouth glued intensely over his raging man meat.

"Go on," he urged breathlessly, "suck my prick off. Go ahead, do me."

Jennifer's prick-hungry mouth slipped further down over his pulsating penis. She massaged his balls as she kept bobbing up and down on his cock head.

"You really enjoy it," he said, full of pride.

It excited him to think that he had trained her. At first, she had been so reluctant to take his prick in her mouth and lick it for him. Now, she was going wild.

"Suck my prick," he panted as he drove into her. "Suck it off."

Jennifer kept massaging Ziggy's huge, swelling balls and working her mouth vigorously up and down the length of his slick, long shaft.

"Eat it," he exclaimed anxiously. "Suck it off. Don't spit it out, either. You've got to keep your lips fastened firmly on my prick. It might become so slick with your saliva that it would slip off at a strategic moment."

All at once, Jennifer began realizing what a difficult task a whore has to keep her lip grip on a saliva-slick cock. Nevertheless, she tried to do her best to keep her lips firm as she felt the young rock star's thick prick plunging down her throat with rapid-fire lust.

"That's really nice, Jennifer," he gasped, "just keep sucking. That's how. Suck, suck, suck it!"

Jennifer instinctively gripped Ziggy's sinewy ass cheeks tightly. She remembered vividly how he had wiggled his butt as he stood at The Forum when he was entertaining the throngs that had turned out to see him. She liked having his bare ass cheeks fucking her face now.

"I'm almost there," he panted as he pumped it to her. "Ohhh, yes. Suck, suck it off."

Ziggy's hot juices were boiling in his balls. He knew that it wouldn't be much longer until he had unloaded.

"Eat it," he exclaimed passionately as he felt his cock penetrating down her throat. "Suck, suck."

Gripping his ass cheeks firmly, Jennifer let her mouth fasten eagerly on his thick penis. It wasn't long before he unloaded. Hot streams of white cum surged down Jennifer's throat.

At first, she nearly gagged. That made the rock star disgusted.

"Damn it, eat it," the horny young man panted as he fucked her face in a wild frenzy of sensual emotion. "Suck, baby, suck off!"

Ziggy's hot balls were exploding. Jennifer could feel sperm hurtling down her throat as she gulped. Her eyes were closed now as she tasted the delicious, thick sperm.

"That was just right," Ziggy patted her head reassuringly as he felt her sucking and swallowing her load.

Ziggy Falcon kept his hot, thick prick probing her throat until he had finished spurting his sperm load. Slowly Ziggy eased his cock from her mouth, and some of his cum dribbled on her lips. Jennifer licked her lips hungrily as she finished him.

8 – The Circle

It had been so terrifying for Susan to see her girlfriend turning on with the London rock idol like this that she finally couldn't resist the urge to do something about it.

"Would you excuse me, John?" she smiled innocently as she got to her feet.

John nodded as he kept his eyes focused on what was happening on the closed-circuit television screen. Some of the office people were now naked and lying in different positions around the room. One young couple was doing a sixty-nine, which excited John Williams, so he wished he could do a sixty-nine with Sally, the new girl he had hired just a week ago. But Sally had her boyfriend with her, and he could see that breaking into what was happening would be difficult. Sally's mouth was slipping up and down her lover's throbbing penis.

In the meantime, Susan stepped into the hall and took the elevator upstairs. She would go to the penthouse and let Ziggy Falcon know he could go to hell and fast.

She walked down the thickly carpeted hallway to the impressive double doors when she arrived at the penthouse suite. However, when she tried the doorknob quietly, it didn't open. It was securely fastened. She realized the only way she could get in would probably be to break the door down, so she turned away. Yet she thought it might not hurt to pound on the door.

Going back, she was just about to pound on the door when she looked at John Williams walking toward her.

"What are you doing up here, Susan?" John demanded, his eyes narrowed to slits.

"Nothing," she said nervously as she put her hands protectively over her purse. '

"You don't kid me," John smiled. "You're worried about Jennifer. Well, forget it. Ziggy Falcon knows how to take care of her. Let's go back and enjoy it on television."

Recognizing that she couldn't make any more protests, Susan felt she might as well agree.

"Sure, why not?" she said lightly, trying to brush aside any suspicions that she was personally jealous of Jennifer.

At this point, Ziggy was telling Jennifer how much he appreciated having sex with her. He ran his fingers through her blond hair affectionately.

"How did I taste?" he smiled.

"Sweet," she whispered.

"That's good," he told her. "I only wish that all my female fans could give me blow jobs like that. You really put fire into your mouth."

It pleased Jennifer that he appreciated what she had done for him, yet she felt a twinge of disgust. She was thinking of Susan Moore and how much she had enjoyed having Susan go down on her pussy.

"A half-hearted cock suck is no damned good," the rock star smiled, "and that's the way a lot of women suck cock. You could be a professional."

A look of disgusted revulsion surfaced on Jennifer's face that indicated to Ziggy he'd said the wrong thing.

"I meant that as a compliment," he told her.

Ziggy was looking at her pussy intently.

"You have such a beautiful body," he told her, reduced to putty now as he gazed affectionately at her crotch area.

Ziggy began massaging her full, ripe bosoms with their taut, rosy-red, erect nipples.

"You're so beautiful," he smiled as he finally reached down to massage her moistening vagina.

Ziggy liked to touch the downy, soft blond pubic hair. He let his fingers slide between the moist pink lips of her pussy. Delightedly he felt her jutting red clit quivering and hard. It was becoming so intensely exciting having his fingers down there that Jennifer was conscious of her juices beginning to flow. The more she became aroused, the more she parted her legs. Her responses to his touch indicated how much she needed sex.

"Now, baby," he told her, "let me return the favor."

A tingle of lurid excitement surged through her being. Jennifer wanted to have him make out with her. He dropped down to her vagina and gripped her ass cheeks. Ziggy pulled her pussy up to his mouth and gently caressed it with his tongue. She enjoyed the sight of him naked over her like this.

"Don't be afraid," he told her as he moved up to stroke her smooth shoulders.

Staring hungrily at her bosoms, Ziggy was anxious to lick her breasts shamelessly.

"Do you mind?" he smiled as he let his hand gently caress her swelling breasts.

All of a sudden, Jennifer found her mental barriers disappearing. She could only respond with delight as a shudder of sexual excitement spread through her, causing her vagina to moisten in anticipation. Ziggy caressed her ripe nipples, letting his thumb slip freely back and forth. Glancing down, Jennifer could see his throbbing cock lurch obscenely, and she knew she must stop him now.

"No, no, don't," she begged him as she tried to wiggle away from his tight grip on her naked body.

But Ziggy was only beginning. He slipped his hands back around her waist. Once more, Jennifer tried to squirm away from him, but Ziggy dropped to his knees. And then she found his hot lips sliding crazily back and forth across her young, quivering, moist mound. His instinctual sexual urges were driving him on as he let his tongue stab mercilessly into her hair-fringed fissure. Jennifer could hardly stand it. Her head rocked from side to side at the devastating thrills she felt when his tongue swept across her juicy crevice with wild abandon. She was overpowered with lusty desire. The rock star had stirred something within her she had never known existed.

This was exactly what Susan Moore was afraid Jennifer would discover. She enjoyed having sex with her so much that she wanted to keep her lush body to herself. The office had turned into an orgy scene. John laughed as he watched them sucking and fucking in different corners of the room.

"We ought to do it on a desk over there," he laughed. "You

could slip out of your clothes, honey, and throw your legs around my neck and let me suck your cunt out."

"Stop it, John," Susan said with some dignity.

At this point, Susan wanted to see exactly what Ziggy was going to do to her girlfriend. It was terrible to see what competition she had to be up against. Ziggy Falcon's huge penis was oozing cum. Apparently, Jennifer had gotten him plenty excited.

Ziggy brought his hand up to Jennifer's moist crotch. He let his middle finger slowly slip into the damp, moist folds of her pink flesh. Jennifer knew this was wrong, but it didn't matter at this moment. The tingling sensation of the rock star's finger prompted her to reach down to grip his head. As she ran her fingers through his thick brown hair, he became more aroused than ever. Jennifer liked what he was doing. Parting the moist folds of her pussy Ziggy licked the quivering cunt flesh. The fragrant aroma of her enticing cuntal opening propelled his tongue into action. He slid it slowly up and down the length of her welcoming vaginal folds.

"Ohhh," Jennifer gasped in erotic frenzy, "stop it, stop it."

Ziggy's fiery tongue was pumping in her pussy in a depraved, obscene way. Anxiously his hands gripped the soft globes of her round buttocks as he buried his face in her crotch, tongue fucking her in pistoning movements. He was probing deeper, ever deeper inside her aroused, throbbing vagina. Tears streaked down Jennifer's cheeks as she trembled with wanton lust. The muscular young rock idol was feasting on the college girl's pussy, his tongue lapping, licking, sucking noisily as he fired her up.

"Ohhh, yes, yes," she gasped, "eat me."

Jennifer was unable to struggle against her own carnal cravings any longer. Whimpering with desire as Ziggy kept his tongue flipping in and out between the pouting pussy lips of her vagina as he lustfully sucked on her erect clitoris, Jennifer was reaching a state of frenzied arousal. Ziggy's teeth bore down gently as he nibbled her there. All of Jennifer's defenses had vanished now.

It was happening now as she gazed down at his head between her legs, her eyes blurred with lusty desire. She pressed back to him as he tongued her. Clutching Ziggy's head, her eyes squeezed shut, her pelvis ground up against his handsome face. She felt his hot tongue lashing out lewdly at her exposed pussy, and then he got his face right in there and sucked until she gushed. The sexual ecstasy that surged through her body now as she was coming in Ziggy's mouth had her gasping in an animalistic frenzy.

"Ohhh, ahhh, I'm cumming, ahhhh!" Jennifer cried out frantically.

The hot, seeping walls of her cunt were being voraciously licked by her lover's lewd tongue.

"Suck me, ohhh, Ziggy-eat me, eat me!"

Ziggy's hot tongue hungrily lapped her up, causing the sensitive area of her clitoris to tingle with delight. His hands clasped her ass cheeks tightly, clenching them as he sucked her cunt noisily. Whether it was the lewd sucking sounds he was making or the wanton way he squeezed her buttocks or the way his teeth bit down on her erect clitoris, she couldn't tell, but the lewd passions within her were rising at this moment.

Jennifer suddenly had a desire for Ziggy's throbbing, long cock to plunge into her pussy. She ached to feel his broad, muscular chest crushing against her soft breast flesh. Totally helpless now, virtue had vanished as her lust-crazed desires took over completely.

When Ziggy noisily finished lapping up her flowing cunt juices, she remembered on the edge of her mind that this was not right. She could never lay any real claim to a rock idol. He belonged to every girl who wanted to bed down with him. Yet she thought to herself as she gazed down at his stone-hard cock, she must have him, too. She didn't want to risk losing the opportunity of knowing him sensually.

Jennifer could imagine what it would be like to have Ziggy's throbbing, long manhood gliding into her hot pussy. She could almost feel her hands reaching out to grip his shoulders, to run down his muscular, firm back to his bare buttocks. Yet it was impossible for this to be actually happening to her. Did she dare say one word? Or was it some illusion that would fade the moment she spoke?

Slowly slipping his tongue from her pussy, Ziggy smiled up at her affectionately. He commanded her to reach for his erect cock. Putting a tentative hand forward, Jennifer gripped his rock-hard penis and squeezed it.

Jennifer had forgotten all about the fact that this was wrong. Moaning ecstatically, she felt his cock harden in her hand grasp. She felt purged of inhibitions, cleansed of depraved guilt feelings. The thrill of anticipation goaded her on. She wanted to feel his throbbing penis sliding into her cuntal sheath.

Ziggy was a man, a man who wanted her sexually. Grasping his huge cock lewdly, she slowly pulled its thick rigidity back and forth. She could feel her own raging genital heat as his lust-bloated balls slapped against her hand as she pumped back and forth with a vigorous hand grip.

"Be honest with yourself, Jennifer," Ziggy smiled at her. "You want me to fuck you, and you want it bad."

Even though Jennifer could admit this to herself, it was not easy to hear Ziggy telling the truth about her own lewd desires. She released her grip on his throbbing cock and turned away, her blond hair attracting him tremendously. Ziggy's eyes swept over her voluptuous curves, and he could see there was nothing to do but fuck her and fuck her fast. He knew he couldn't wait.

"Come on, baby," he told her, "get set. You're gonna get fucked."

She felt the throb of his huge cock as he pressed close to her.

"You want to feel my cock in you, Jennifer, don't you?" he whispered sensuously. "Just stretch out on the bed. Let's fuck and get it off now."

At this point, she felt his hands sweep forward to caress and tease her bosoms, pinching the taut nipples recklessly. Again, she felt waves of sensuous need rushing through her body. The more his hands touched her, the more desire was winning out. Gently sweeping down to her hair-fringed fissure, he inserted his middle finger again. The pouting lips of her pussy gave way to the delicious finger sliding inside of her. A small moan of animalistic lust issued from her throat as she squeezed her eyes shut, enjoying his touch, even more, when she shut off her senses, except for his luridly probing finger in her.

"Stretch out," he whispered.

Sliding his fingers from her pussy lips as she started to move forward, Ziggy watched her lie there naked beneath him. The London rock star was quite a contrast to the stunning young college graduate who lay underneath him, her eyes looking lustfully up at him. Straddling her, Jennifer felt the hugeness of his fleshy hardness sliding impatiently back and forth across her quivering cuntal slit. It made her tingle to feel the blood-engorged head of his throbbing cock waiting to lurch forward into her moist pussy hole.

Jennifer knew the head of his cock could ignite all the fiery passions pent up in her young body. She had to have it in her now, but he was going to make her beg for it. Suddenly, she felt she couldn't go through with it.

"No, no, I can't," she cried out with urgency.

Her vision was blurred as hot tears stained her cheeks. Jumping away from him, she ran across the room. That only ignited Ziggy all the more.

"Hey, I like a girl who puts up a fight," he told her. "Not many of them will. There's a lot of thrill when you think you're raping a girl."

Looking at him in horror, Jennifer Davis realized that he was sincere. Trying to reason with him wasn't going to work.

"You're sick," she told him.

Grabbing her crudely, Ziggy lustfully shoved her down again.

"Some women like to be raped," Ziggy Falcon chuckled.

He got on top of Jennifer now and insisted that she reach down and grasp his rigid penis.

"No," she complained.

It aroused Ziggy to slap her face.

"When I tell you to do something," he said with an animalistic look in his eyes, "you do it!"

Reaching forward now, she gripped his rigid penis and stroked up and down on his hard shaft. It aroused him all the more to see droplets of white cum oozing from the small slit at the crown of his cock.

"Go ahead," he commanded, "guide my prick into your cunt."

There was something about Ziggy's virile, masculine voice giving her a lewd command that aroused her masochistic, passionate feeling. Without saying a word, she reached out to grip his cock and guide it to her cunt lips. She felt the tip of his penis slip inside her moist vagina. Whispering with delight, he held his breath, luxuriating in the intoxicating sensations of having his throbbing man meat sliding into her fiery hot cunt hole.

He closed his eyes as the pulsating flesh entered her cuntal sheath. Moaning throatily, Jennifer felt his impaling thickness sliding into her. All the shame was gone, and her body trembled and quaked. He was humiliating her, forcing her to be his love slave. As she felt him guiding his manhood into her pussy portals, she begged, "Oh, Ziggy, fuck me, fuck me."

All inhibitions had vanished with her own carnal lustful

desire. She splayed her legs wider, granting Ziggy easy access to her open cunt. Lewdly her muscular young lover slowly eased his huge shaft into her moistly heated cunt. She groaned as she felt the thick, blood-engorged head of his penis sliding inside of her. The elastic opening of her pussy gave way, and Ziggy suddenly realized he was fucking a virgin. This got him so excited he really rammed it to her.

"Ohhh, ahhh, aaaahhh, aaaahhhh," she whimpered as his huge cock tip drove past her tight cuntal opening.

Jennifer wanted it. Every fucking inch of his cock meat. He was busting her cherry, and she loved it.

Nothing else mattered now.

"Fuck me-fuck me," she cried out passionately. "I want it-I want every fucking inch!"

Grasping his shoulders, she begged for it.

"Oh, Ziggy, screw me!"

Hot tears scalded her cheeks as Jennifer's girlfriend, Susan Moore, watched what was happening on the television screen. John observed this out of the corner of his eye but said nothing. He sensed that Susan felt guilty about inviting young, innocent Jennifer to the rock idol's opening night.

"If you don't want to look at it," John said under his breath, "for God's sake, get out of here."

"Not a bad idea," Susan said, her voice quivering with emotion.

She left the office where everyone was involved in some kind of sex act. It was a disgusting orgy, and she wanted out of there. Going into her own office, she closed the door behind her and locked it carefully. Walking over to her desk, she suddenly found herself sobbing uncontrollably. There was the city spread out before her in all of its splendor. And all around her was the posh elegance that she had worked so hard to obtain. But it meant nothing.

Her beautiful female lover was being assaulted, raped by a sex brute named Ziggy Falcon. Sure, he could turn women on across two continents. But what the fuck did it mean to her? It only meant that keeping Jennifer for herself would be all the more difficult. Once Jennifer had tasted the fantastic thrills of having sex with a man, Susan Moore was certain she would never come back to her. This was tormenting her mind, driving her almost to the point of frenzy.

Finally, she placed her head down on her desk and quietly sobbed to herself.

Little did Jennifer Davis realize how her conduct affected her girlfriend, Susan Moore. For she had no way of knowing that someone had inadvertently flipped a switch that had turned on the closed-circuit television in the penthouse suite where Jennifer and Ziggy Falcon were having sex.

All of the lustful desires within her were coming into play now. Desperately, she needed to satisfy her carnal cravings. Ziggy really rammed it to her, and she loved it. He knew exactly what he was doing. Tantalizing her, teasing her, and making her beg for his huge shaft was all part of his erotic pleasure. His eyes froze with fear, however, as she looked up at him. He looked like a changed man. He was no longer the handsome young rock idol. He was a sex-crazy, lustful, wild man. Obviously, he was lost in Jennifer's bodily appeal.

An evil look surfaced on his determined face as he shoved

forward. Ziggy was hovering over Jennifer now, and she was helpless beneath him. The pulsating head of his throbbing cock disappeared into her hot pussy hole. He shoved forward, his chest crushing down hard against her ripe, rounded bosoms. Ziggy rammed his thick prick forward with all of his muscular strength and his thighs and buttocks. Jennifer felt his throbbing, long cock gliding into her cunt in a pistoning movement.

She soon became thrilled at the way he slashed and ravaged her tender flesh. It was amazing how pleasureful a cock could be in her cunt. There had been a fear about having sex for the first time. It didn't matter that she was a virgin; she learned at last. This only seemed to turn Ziggy on all the more. Maybe some of the girls that he screwed before had done it so many times they were worn out or loose. But she was tight and tremendous, and Ziggy loved it.

The wildly gyrating Ziggy was beginning to sweat profusely. Looking up at him, Jennifer smiled. He was pumping hard now.

"Ohhh, ahhh, it's too much, Ziggy," she cried out impulsively. "I can't stand it."

Ziggy's rock-hard cock tunneled in now into her tight vagina. The assault on her narrow passageway made her feel as though she was coming apart under the sharp impact of his driving prick meat. But he wouldn't stop now. His lust-contorted features, the sweaty body, and the weight of his chest crushing on her breasts, combined with his fiery, plunging penis driving up hard against her cervix, thrilled her almost to climax. Her hands reached for his broad shoulders.

She let her hands slip smoothly back and forth across his shoulders and gently began massaging up and down his back. Jennifer loved having the entire length of his shaft filling her belly. She couldn't seem to get enough of him. Ziggy's heavily veined, rock-hard cock was plunging vigorously against the walls of her cunt which clasped around his sliding shaft in a rhythmic, responsive gripping movement.

"Fuck me, fuck me," she panted passionately, her fingernails clawing down his muscular back until he was bleeding.

But it didn't matter. It only fired him to fuck her all the more. Her pussy muscles steadily contracted as his huge shaft continued riding her. By clasping and releasing her grip on his thrusting tool, she could feel the shiver of sexual electricity flashing up and down her spine. Her body was on fire to be fucked. She had to have him.

"Ohhh, ahhh, yes, yesssss, like that!" she begged as she felt him deliberately driving his man-meat first in one direction and then the other.

Jennifer ground helplessly, lost in lust, unable to catch her breath as he savagely fucked her. She could feel her narrow pussy channel being stretched wider by Ziggy's driving cock stabs. He burrowed in deeply, throwing his ass in gear as he furiously fucked her.

"What a beautiful virgin," he exclaimed. "You really have thrilled me."

Her hands reached out to grip the firm, round globes of Ziggy's ass cheeks. She squeezed his sinewy buttocks, closing her eyes in sensual ecstasy as he rode into her with plunging, writhing cock stabs. Heatedly, her body twitched beneath him. She could see his thick, fleshy penis as he pulled up. Then he was driving back between her legs, her tender cunt lips stretched tightly now as the rubbery rim clasped firmly around his glistening, stabbing cock. He watched it plunge in and out of her slowly as he changed the tempo of his penis stabs.

It stimulated him to see Jennifer's body twitching beneath him. Apparently, she wanted him to ride his prick in her all the way, to feel its throbbing hugeness plunging into her without mercy. She wanted to feel his balls slapping lewdly against her tightly clenched, quivering ass cheeks.

"Fuck me, fuck me, Ziggy," she panted, her voice trembling with passionate feeling. "Let me feel it."

His skewering prick drove in and out of her with a slow, hypnotic rhythm that ignited her cunt again. She began pumping back in perfect time to his driving cock jabs. He thrust the full throbbing length of his lusty male member into her, feeling the cuntal clasp of her vaginal walls as she gripped his stabbing shaft. Then he slowly withdrew his deeply embedded cock, pulling out gently and letting it rest on the wet, swollen lips of her pussy.

Once more, he wanted to see that burning glaze of sensual desire in her lustful eyes. Ziggy wanted to hear her beg for it. Jennifer's face contorted in a passion-driven desire as his cock rested there.

"Fuck me... fill me with your prick," she gasped.

The rock star rammed forward now with all of his savage, sexual drive. The full throbbing length of his cock drove into her helpless cunt, deeper and deeper. Over and over, he thrust into her helpless cunt, deeper and deeper. Over and over, he thrust his man meat into her. With each thudding stab, he could feel her pumping back to meet him. Reaching underneath her now, Ziggy clasped the full cheeks of her smooth, satiny ass.

He cupped her buttocks hotly in the palms of his hands, squeezing them as he continued driving his cruel cock into her moist, clasping cunt. Her face flushed, indicating the mixed pain and pleasure she was feeling at the same instant. She looked up at Ziggy's muscular shoulders, firm-set jaw, and erotic blazing eyes, feeling helpless. He forced her legs over now, so he could have deeper access to her cunt. Ziggy's only concern was his own pleasure. At this angle, he could obtain deeper penetration. Jennifer felt the huge cock pistoning in and out of her cunt. His bloated balls slapped lewdly against her anus every time he drilled her.

She could feel a whiff of cool air in her ass crack as he spread her legs to obtain still deeper penetration into her pussy. His chest pressed down on her, keeping her pinned in this uncomfortable position. His hands gripped her breasts, squeezing them crudely, pinching them, hurting them as he continued ravaging her tender female flesh.

It had become so stimulating to John Williams to watch the different members of his office carrying on sexually that he figured Susan ought to be with him. Noticing that she had left him, he went to her office to see what was happening.

Observing the door was locked, he pounded on it vigorously. He became concerned when there was still no answer.

At last, however, Susan realized she had to answer. Going

to the door, she finally opened it. Looking up at John, she asked him what he wanted.

"I think we ought to go back into the office and organize an orgy," he told her.

"What are you talking about?" she demanded.

"It got me so excited just watching Ziggy fuck Jennifer. I figured we ought to start a real office orgy. Let's have a suck circle."

Before Susan could say anything, he was pulling her by the hand into the other room. When they returned to the office party, the boss smiled at the different workers. He figured it would be fun to organize them.

"Let's form a cock-sucking circle," John suggested. "We'll watch Ziggy fucking Jennifer while we're having our suck circle."

Patricia, who was new at the record company, didn't know what he was talking about. John immediately began passing out grass.

"Get high, everybody," he suggested, "and take off your clothes. We can throw towels down on the floor and form our wild suck circle. Push the desks to the side."

Soon, the weed was being distributed, and the desks were being pushed to the side of the room. It took little imagination for Patricia to catch on quickly as to what was expected. The men of the office staff were taking off their clothes, and so were the women. When the office floor was cleared, towels were placed in a circle.

"You'll catch on, Patricia," John smiled. "Just grab your date by his balls, pull him over to a towel, and tell him to spread his legs so you can go down on him."

Patricia's lover, Robert, was at her side, standing there naked, his huge cock quivering.

"Grab it, Patricia," he smiled, "and suck on it." Patricia reached for his cock reluctantly. However, she realized it could be terribly exciting when she felt it quivering in her hand.

At the same time, John was organizing the arrangement of the towels on the floor so they would form a perfect circle. The room had almost no light except the large wall television. The closed-circuit TV performance of the London rock idol carrying on with the innocent young college graduate provided just the kind of erotic stimulation everyone needed.

"Men, on your backs," John commanded as he finished sliding out of his shorts and going over to a towel.

Much as she hated to, Susan Moore felt she had to comply with John's sordid request. Any girl who didn't go along with his wild ideas on sex would be instantly fired.

It didn't take her long to realize John was a demon.

John lay on his back, and so did the other male members of the office staff of Empire Vinyl Records. They were paired off perfectly now as John started the cock-sucking circle.

"The object is to see how long you can hold it, men," he explained. "You've got to keep your juice in your balls as long as possible. The girls must seek to get every man to shoot his wad. When I say 'change cocks,' that means that you switch to the next one. Come on, let's go."

9 – It Sucks

Patricia looked at her naked lover, Robert. It wasn't easy for her to crouch down between his wide-spread thighs. Robert was a blond, muscular, athletic man. He propped his head back on a couple of pillows from the nearby sofa. At this angle, he could watch as Patricia gripped his quivering cock and began licking the tip. It was a first night at an orgy for Patricia, and it wasn't easy to bring herself to perform such wild sex.

"Now, Patricia," Robert grinned, "pretend it's a lollipop and lick it. You'll get to love it. It just takes a little training."

Patricia closed her eyes. That bothered Robert. He was proud of his penis and felt she ought to watch what was happening.

"Keep your eyes open, honey," he told her, "and lick it. Look at it. See it quiver as your tongue slips over the head of the shaft."

Patricia agreed. Her tongue swept out over the crown of his massive, bulbous cock head.

"Now suck on it," he insisted, "and suck it good."

Sliding her mouth over his shaft, she started sucking vigorously. It pleased Robert to see that she was an avid learner.

"The trick is," he explained, "to suck under the cock. That's it. The sensitive glans portion of the penis is where it feels the best."

Patricia was getting her instructions in cock sucking. And as she looked at the other girls who were going down on their dates in the circle that had been formed on the floor, she marveled at the loud, slurping, sucking sounds they all seemed to be making.

The girl beside her was sparing nothing. She was going up and down the meaty, long shaft. And at the same time, she was massaging the man's hairy, swelling testicles. It was quite obvious to her how aroused he was becoming. The young man reached out and gripped her head, forcing her down over his penis.

Patricia trembled as the burning length of Robert's cock shoved down her throat. She wondered how much of this she could take.

"I'm almost there," he told her, "so take it easy."

He loved the sensation of the wetness of her mouth engulfing his pecker. Her lips fastened frantically on his throbbing penis as she hungrily tried to milk him.

"That's it," he told her, "suck cock."

Looking out of the corner of her eye, she could see the girl next to her going down on her young lover. It was interesting to notice the different ways the girls gave heads.

Linda was licking her lips as she let her pink tongue tip slid over Jim's cock. Linda was to the right of her. And she was watching. Linda lowered her head and tenderly licked the head of her lover's rigid cock. Jim grinned at Linda and was pleased at what she was doing.

"Oh, wow, Linda," he exclaimed, "go right ahead."

Jim let his eyes roam over the different girls who were going up and down on their lover's penis. It was an erotically stimulating sight that made his body tingle with excitement.

She lowered her head and licked the swollen tip of his penis. It was as if lightning had struck him there. Jim looked at her nakedness. He saw Linda's breasts quivering as her head slid up and down on his swollen rod. Linda's red lips seemed to stick to the slick skin of his cock, causing an extra pang of pleasure to surge through his body. It was hard for him to accept. The action was so stimulating it wasn't easy to play the game of keeping his balls in tow.

"Ohhh, Linda," he groaned as his hands dug into her hair and held her head still while he savored the sensation of his penis throbbing in her mouth.

The nudge of Linda's hot tongue lashing against his cock head was electrifying, and he wanted to cum right then, blowing his load of milky goo into her sucking mouth. But he held back. Linda's lips slipped eagerly up and down her lover's rod. She had enjoyed cock sucking ever since she learned it from her little brother. But this was even more stimulating because everybody was doing it in the cock-sucking circle.

The wild, plunging motions of Jim's pecker between her sweet, full lips caused a burning itchy sensation in her crotch. She loved the feel and taste of Jim's penis in her mouth. It was delicious and stimulating. The heavy flavor of his cum seeping from the end and filling her mouth was nectar to her lips.

"Don't suck it off yet," Jim warned her. "I've got to have at least two women go down on me tonight."

She enjoyed having his big prick riding in and out of her mouth. It thrilled her the way he was plunging with such enthusiasm. She wanted to suck and fuck him completely.

With each stroke of her mouth on Jim's rigid, throbbing penis, it was driving him closer and closer to orgasm.

"Don't do it so fast," Jim begged.

His fingers tightened around Linda's head, entwining themselves in her hair as he guided her rhythm. He loved the feel of her lips ringing his pulsating pecker. Jim was ecstatic about the hot friction of her lips as he watched her head move up and down his turgid penis.

Linda pulled her head up, and his pecker pulled from the softness of her mouth.

"Do you want me to quit?" she asked, noticing how he slowed her down.

"No way," he told her. "Suck me, baby, but just don't swallow it yet. There's enough suck in that cock for two or three women."

Once more, she let his big, thick prick slip into her mouth. Jim guided the head of his cock where he wanted it. He directed his heated prick to her lips and practically forced her mouth down over it. He sighed as he felt her swallowing his sex organ in her mouth.

"Ohhh," he panted. "Suck cock. Suck it."

She couldn't talk. The huge, throbbing cock enclosed within her lips made it impossible. She could barely breathe. Jim was frantic with lust and couldn't stop now. He had to have her mouth pumping up and down on his ready-to-erupt prick. Just then, John Williams, the president of Empire Vinyl Records, forced Susan Moore off his pecker.

"Switch cocks," John called out. "Ohh, it's just in time. You nearly got my rocks off, Susan baby."

Linda reluctantly pulled her mouth off Jim's prick. And Patricia moved over to grasp Jim's huge, throbbing penis as the entire cock-sucking circle changed cocks and continued sucking.

Jim was pleased that John had called the cock-suck change just in time.

At this moment, he watched as a smoldering young girl went down on him. Running his fingers through her hair, he remembered he didn't even know her name.

"What's your name, honey?" he smiled as he watched the redhead going down on his throbbing manhood.

The fair-skinned, green-eyed girl slipped her ruby lips off his shaft and smiled up at him, "Don't you remember me, boss? I'm Tracy. You hired me one night when you visited me at a sex parlor."

John Williams preferred to keep his girls from revealing their backgrounds. He chided her. Laughter erupted as the people on both sides of him heard Tracy reveal her past.

"Oh, yes," he joked, "Tracy, you're real good at head. You've got a cute ass, too. I remember I fucked you up the asshole the first time I met you."

Tracy grinned as she gripped his manhood and began licking and sucking on him again. He didn't want her to suck him completely, but he was eager to have her go down on him and give him a wild mouth trip.

Her head bobbed up and down as she felt John's sex explosion gathering in his balls. Tracy wanted it. She wanted to taste and smell and drink the boss's sperm. It couldn't be much longer, she was certain until he pumped it into her sucking mouth.

"Oh, I love it," he told her. "Now you're sucking. That's how it's done. Suck, suck."

He pumped it hard into her mouth. And she grabbed at his buttocks and began fingering his asshole. When he was just about to cum she slipped her mouth off his prick and looked up at him.

"Don't stop now," he begged her. "Keep sucking. You're doing it really well."

Her finger gliding up John's tight anus stimulated and aroused him. He always enjoyed having a prostate massage. He also liked the way she clasped the massive base of his prick as she went up and down on his throbbing pole. It pleased her to feel the purple head of it ready to erupt.

"Suck," John commanded her in a hypnotic voice. "Suck my prick."

The thought of having him shoot his wad was causing her mouth to water. His testicles swung between his legs, and then she had the strange desire to lick his balls and fondle them with her tongue. She wanted to suck them in her mouth.

Slipping her mouth off his prick, she went down on his cock and licked his balls. The next thing he knew, she had slipped her finger from his asshole and was clutching his ass cheeks as she grabbed his cock and started jerking as she sucked on his balls.

"Ohhh, baby," he gasped, "don't do that. You're getting me so excited I'll shoot my load. If I'm going to go off, I want a hot mouth over my prick."

It didn't take her long to slip her mouth over his shaft and start sucking hard.

"Suck me, suck me," he begged. "Suck off."

John's penis was buried within Tracy's wanton mouth. The palms of her hands massaged his ass cheeks as she sucked. Her lower lip excited him as she slipped his cock out of her mouth and tantalizingly sucked his head again.

"Now you're doing it," he told her. "Suck my prick off."

John's eyes feasted on the erotic sight all around him. Each office girl was going down on the men who worked there. It pleased him to think that he could get them all to obey. And Tracy was kneading and stroking his buttocks and thighs as her hot tongue swept over the tip of his penis.

"Come on and suck," he begged. "Suck off."

Suddenly he jerked his massive cock dripping with saliva from her mouth. He told her that it was too much.

"Change cocks," John called out as his eyes focused once more on what was happening on the television screen. "Look at them go," he exclaimed as he saw what was happening.

Ziggy Falcon was ramming his prick into Jennifer Davis with such savage force she was twisting her head from side to side. He was letting go now with a wild-driving cock jab.

"Come on, baby," he told her, "grab it with your cunt."

His hands reached out to caress her breasts as he stabbed his prick without mercy in her gripping, tight twat. Squeezing the pink nipples of her breasts, he watched her as she groaned in pain and twisted her head back and forth.

"Now you're fucking," he exclaimed excitedly.

"Fuck, fuck."

She fought back only hard enough to keep him interested. And when she could take no more, she moved in and circled his hips with her thighs, enjoying it enormously.

"You're gonna get screwed," he told her as he rammed in, her firm, bloated balls slapping lewdly against her anus every time he drilled her cunt.

Ziggy pressed down hard now, enjoying it enormously. Their entwined bodies struggled for release. They both wanted to experience that peak of passion, that lust-crazed moment when they would cum together. Her body pitched back to his meaty, throbbing cock stabs. She reached for his ass cheeks and squeezed them with wild abandon as he rode his hot, pumping shaft into her moist, slurping cunt.

"Ohhh, ahhh, yes, yes, yes," Jennifer gasped again and again. "Ram it to me, baby. I want to feel it. Every fucking inch of it!"

Ziggy continued driving his cock steadily in her wetly sucking cunt. Parting his ass cheeks, she fingered his tight anus. He enjoyed the sensation of her finger slipping up his tight anus while he rammed it into her. With hard, long lunges, he went on thrusting his surging prick into her grasping cunt. Savagely he propelled his pulsating penis into her. Jennifer's heated breasts heaved and quivered, her hard nipples pressing against his chest as he brushed back and forth.

In the meantime, the cock-sucking circle was deriving inspiration from the giant television screen. They would keep their eyes focused on the TV screen as they would go up and down on their lovers' throbbing man meat. It gave them the sensation as if they, too, were being fucked by the London rock idol, and this doubled their pleasure.

The television screen showed Ziggy Falcon was a real stud. All that meant anything at this erotic moment was his passionate urge to cum. Ziggy continued driving his thick, pulsating shaft in and out of her pussy, driving it all the way inside her. Jennifer quivered under him now, stabbing her finger all the way up his hot, tight asshole as he felt his cock driving into her with unrelenting fiery stabs.

His hands urgently gripped her breasts, impatiently squeezing the nipples until they were blood red. Then he pulled off, driving his cock-meat in all the way. He exploded gushingly into her cunt.

"Ohhh, ahhh, fuck, fuck," she cried out in wanton passion.

Jennifer slipped her finger from his tight asshole. She wound her sweaty legs around Ziggy's legs as she pumped back up to meet him.

"Ahhh, ohhh, I'm coming," Jennifer groaned as she joined the rock idol in juicing.

Her hands gripped his sinewy, bare buttocks, squeezing and pinching his ass cheeks as he kept shooting inside of her.

At that very moment, John Williams found the girl who was going down on him was doing such a superb job that he couldn't hold back. He wanted to get his rocks off at the same instant Ziggy had because he had become overpowered by the erotic excitement of seeing him fuck young Jennifer.

"Suck, baby, suck," he whispered anxiously as the young girl went up and down on his throbbing man meat. "Suck off," he exclaimed anxiously. "Oh, baby, do it for me."

The blond-haired young girl sucked faster, bringing him to a climax quicker.

"Oh, baby, suck it-suck it off!"

The young blonde enjoyed having the boss's hard column of flesh in her fingers. It jerked to her touch as she pinched at its base. She could feel the hot blood pumping crazily through it.

"I'm gonna flood your face with it," he told her. "Now suck."

Recognizing that she had to please him made it difficult. But she knew what was expected.

"I'm gonna fuck your face like you've never been fucked before," he panted as he pumped his throbbing penis down her throat.

He looked at her as she labored over his stiff rod, her eyes flashing with mounting passion, her tongue flicking back and forth across the tip of his cock.

It wasn't going to be much longer before he was shooting. His hips raised up off the towel as she clasped his ass cheeks.

"I want you to eat it," he told her.

Passionately she went up and down on his penis.

"Ohhh," he gasped as he sent his prick all the way down her throat, almost choking her on his cock meat.

The girls recognized that when the boss wanted to get his rocks off, they could continue sucking. And each girl was anxious to have the tingling, thrilling excitement of swallowing the cum load of the guy that she was making it with. Hungrily the blonde girl went up and down on John's penis. Tears of joy streamed from her eyes as she realized he was ready to shoot.

"Keep your lips fastened on my prick," he begged her. "I don't want you to lose any."

At this moment, he reached out and gripped her head.

"Suck it, baby," John boomed again. "Suck my big prick."

The young girl sucked and licked at his fleshy member embedded in her mouth, creating a vacuum of lust that brought a moan of delight from her boss. She was salivating so much now that his cock slid back and forth almost effortlessly, tiny rivulets of drool trailing from the corners of her tightly rounded lips to run down the rigid stock into the wiry pubic bush of his loins. She sucked until her throat muscles ached with strain.

"Come on, baby, eat my meat. Suck it."

She did and more, the tip of her busy pink tongue dipping sweetly into the split at the end of John's glans, her long-nailed finger milking and teasing the heavy sac that housed the testicles of the man who was giving her a powerful fuck.

He began slamming forward, shoving the huge cock' down her throat. John held her bobbing head more tightly as she coughed and sputtered delightedly with each powerful instroke, and the lust-purpled head of his cock fucked rhythmically into her throat. He delighted in watching her red-rimmed lips clasping eagerly around his turgid, blue-veined shaft as her mouth muscles wearied and her warm oral cavity became accustomed to the size of his pistoning shaft. Her lush lips slipped up and down the slippery head of his shaft, creating such a vacuum that John knew he was coming in a second.

"Ohhh, baby, suck cock," he screamed. "I'm coming. Eat it."

Desperately, thrilled to the very core of her being, the young girl sucked and swallowed to keep from gagging as her mouth filled and emptied. He was an absolute reservoir of sticky white semen. John strained forward again and emptied the last of his cum deep inside her mouth, then released his grip from her hair as he felt himself deflating inside the obscenely flooded hole of her mouth.

His prick slipped from her mouth, and then he could see sticky strings of his hot sperm still connecting her face to his penis even though it was now inches from her lips. The girl's breathing was heavy and wet, as though her mouth and nose were completely covered with moisture.

She sat back on her haunches in front of the panting and exhausted rock-record kingpin.

"Was I a good cock eater?" she asked him, her eyes sparkling merrily, her nose wrinkled up in a child-like tease.

John looked down at her and winked.

"You are a very talented young lady," he assured her.

"Gee, thanks," she smiled.

John realized he had become so carried away with his own frenzied eruption he had forgotten that he was to call time to change cocks.

"Change cocks," John called out.

One man had gotten it off just watching John. It had stimulated him so much to see John get so carried away that his sperm was unloaded in the sucking girl's mouth. But the rest of the men were waiting for that moment when John would cry out, having become so absorbed in what he was doing they almost forgot about their own cock sucking.

In the meantime, Ziggy Falcon was pulling his prick out of Jennifer's cunt. Jennifer looked up at him in amazement.

"You've still got a hard," Jennifer told him.

The cock-sucking circle was watching the television screen on the closed-circuit TV with such avid interest that they all erupted in laughter as they looked at the London rock idol's throbbing cock swinging between his legs as he went over to the bar in the penthouse suite and mixed a drink for himself and the young girl.

Jennifer looked at Ziggy's cock in amazement as he sat down on the sofa beside her again. Her eyes were huge with inviting and sensuous desire.

"You're amazing," she told him.

"Why do you say that?" he asked, knowing full well what she meant.

"I'll tell you why," she smiled. "It's because you still have a hard-on."

At that point, he didn't hesitate to tell her what he wanted to do. He grinned silently and sipped his drink.

"Why don't you play with it?" he asked her. "Just pull on it."

Reaching over, she gripped his huge, throbbing penis.

"Wow!" Ziggy told her. "You sure know how to play with me."

She massaged his balls with one hand and pulled on his throbbing manhood with the other.

"They're sure enjoying it," Don called out, looking at the screen action in the office.

This bothered Karen, who was sucking on him. "Quit watching them," she told him. "That's perverted to look at people fucking."

That brought a round of laughter. Karen was only egotistical and wanted all of Don's attention directed to the excitement of her cock sucking.

Don insisted that she lick his ass as well.

"That isn't included," Karen included.

"If I say so, it is," Don demanded.

Don forced Karen to go down on his ass. She held his round, sinewy buttocks in her hands and then parted them.

"Oh, that's nice," Don told her as the sweet desire of an ass-licking swept through him.

She began maneuvering her finger in his asshole, and then she let her tongue slide along his ass crack.

"Yes," he told her as his buttocks churned, "thrust it up."

Pumping her tongue up his asshole caused Don to blurt, "Baby, you're driving me ape."

Turned on now, Don grabbed his prick and jacked off while she ass-licked. That gave an idea to a couple of other lovers who were making it.

Patricia was forced to pull her mouth off Jay's cock and lick his balls and then stick her tongue right up his rectum. Jay lay back, thrilled by the sensation of the rim job.

"Whee," he gasped gleefully, "everybody's sucking prick or licking ass."

It was true. The entire office force was down on the floor

in a circle on towels. And each one of them was busy with their own wild sexual connection. He moaned with pleasure as she guided her tongue right up his tight anus. The thrill of getting her to do something so degrading provided him with enormous pleasure. Don watched.

"Look at her suck," he smiled.

At the same time, Ziggy Falcon was speaking with Jennifer Davis about another kind of sex.

"Some people would say I have perverse desires," he told her.

"Oh, you mustn't criticize yourself," Jennifer Davis insisted.

Her lover and ex-roommate Susan Moore heard this. Susan could never reveal what she was thinking, but it bothered her that Jennifer was becoming so sloppy in her morals that she would permit Ziggy Falcon to do anything and not recognize what a morally perverse man he was.

Ziggy was telling Jennifer to stretch out on her stomach because he wanted to give her a massage.

"I think that would be a very relaxing thing for you to do to me," she said as she released her grip on his proud penis and gleefully stretched out on her stomach.

At this point, he massaged her back gently. He pressed on the nerve centers up and down her spine, and for the first time, she realized how tired she actually was. She had become so aroused with all of the sexual excitement that she hadn't recognized she had been up for such a long period of time.

"Just relax, honey," he told her as his hands insinuated themselves around her bosoms.

New kinds of thrills were going through her body now

as the rock idol treated her to a tongue lashing up and down her back.

"What are you doing?" Jennifer giggled.

Ziggy Falcon paid no attention to her question. He clutched the resilient globes of ass flesh and parted them. Then he let his tongue slip to her ass crack. When her anus was exposed, he suddenly plunged his tongue right up her rectum. Horrified that he would do such a thing, she told him to stop. But Ziggy blissfully sucked on her ass and fingered her pussy at the same time.

"Ohhh, that does feel so good," she admitted. "Go ahead and suck on it."

The office cock-sucking circle was continuing even though John couldn't take any more sucking. He realized that soon he would have to switch to pussy eating. That would provide him with the pleasure that he wanted. But he enjoyed watching one of the new men working for him.

Tony Bacchi was stretched out a few feet away, and a young girl was blushing as she went down on his huge meaty cock. He watched the nervous office girl pulling the thick, blood-engorged penis of Tony to her mouth. When John called out the cock sucking should begin again, she went on with the performance. Reaching up, she played with his awesome penis.

"Go down on it," Tony told her.

Reaching down, Tony gripped her head, forcing her over his throbbing, long cock. Excitedly he told her to suck. Her lips went around his lusty shaft. How long it was, the young girl thought to herself. To get it all in her mouth was not going to be easy as Tony must have the biggest hunk of cock meat of any man in the office.

Tony did not instantly slam it down her throat. He knew he had to take it easy with all of that man meat.

"Relax," he told her. "Just take it slow."

Her lips opened as she accepted his raging cock. Her fingers softly caressed his balls. Tony loved the way she toyed with his testicles.

"Now lick it," he told her.

The office girl's soft, pink lips moved sensuously on Tony's rod, and her tongue ran tantalizingly under the tender glans portion of his penis.

"Oh, baby," Tony exclaimed as he felt a shudder of sensual delight surging through his body. "Come on, baby," he told her, "have a good suck."

It was strange how his lewdness didn't bother her. At this moment, she wanted to feel his throbbing, long cock sliding smoothly in and out of her mouth. At the same time, Tony reached out to grip her bosom. He squeezed them tightly and pinched her nipples.

"Come on, baby," he panted in heated passion, "suck it. Suck."

Tony plunged his cock roughly down her throat, and she accepted all of him.

"Ohhh, that's how I like it," he gasped as he kept pumping it down her throat.

She was almost choking now.

"Suck, suck," Tony demanded.

When she was about to bring him off, he pulled away, shoving her head.

"Take it easy," he told her. "Save some for the next girl. Once it shoots off, it won't be hard."

The young girl laughingly chided him.

"Ziggy Falcon stayed hard," she quipped.

He smiled as he looked down at her.

"You can suck it a couple of seconds more," he permitted her.

Her pink tongue slipped over his penis. And then he began fucking fiercely forward, the full length of his cock driving savagely. She could feel him ramming it down her throat, and she almost choked as he rode his prick in her face.

"Keep sucking me," he panted.

Closing her eyes, she focused on the fantastic long prick sliding into her mouth. Burning pangs of heated passion raged uncontrollably in her belly. The velvety warmth of her cunt was stimulated now. She wished that Tony's tongue was pumping furiously in her pussy.

"I want you to suck me off," Tony panted. "Suck me, suck me."

At this point, he cried out more passionately, "Eat it, eat it."

Tony exploded. He filled her mouth to overflowing with his sticky white semen. His heavy, rock-hard cock was still unloading as she swallowed hard to keep from choking.

It excited John just to see Tony's fiery, plunging rod filling the young girl's face with his sperm. The semen dripped from the corner of her lips as his lengthy, thick shaft finished fucking her face.

"Change cocks," John laughed, "and next time around we'll change cunts."

Reluctantly the young office girl pulled her mouth off Tony Bacchi's cock.

"You really enjoyed it, didn't you?" Tony grinned as he reached out and pulled her chin up so he could look into her eyes.

The girl smiled as she admitted how much she enjoyed having his huge, throbbing cock sliding down her throat with his fiery, plunging movements.

Once more, the cock-sucking circle was changing. The next man in line, who looked at her, smiled warmly. Brian knew that this young chick was a natural, instinctive cock eater.

"Hey, I hope you give me as good a suck as you gave him," Brian grinned.

Promising him that she would, she gripped Brian's huge shaft. The blood-engorged head of his cock indicated to her that he was ready to cum. Letting her tongue slide over the meaty tip of his penis, she finally began sucking.

"Suck off," he told her. "Go down on it."

She went up and down on his shaft, getting him so excited that he was shaking. Firmly she gripped his ass globes and squeezed them as she bobbed up and down on his blood-engorged cock.

"Suck off," he demanded. "That's what I want you to do. Eat my cock, eat it."

Industriously she sucked, and she knew that it couldn't be much longer until she was rewarded, for she could taste him starting to cum. Gripping her head, he forced her down on his penis.

"Suck it off," he commanded, "suck off."

Hot sperm splashed down her throat.

"Ohhh," he gasped as he gripped her head, "that's what I like. Now you're sucking. Keep it up."

When she had finished giving him a hot cock sucking, she eased her mouth off his penis, then flicked at his balls and sucked on his asshole. He held his ass up for her in the offering. She gripped the globes of his sinewy buttocks and closed her eyes as she slipped her tongue right up his rectum.

"Ohhh," he groaned in erotic delight as she rimmed him.

10 – Hired

As John Williams went into his private office to pick up the phone, he was still stark naked. Sitting on the edge of the desk, he reached for his phone and answered the call.

"Yes?" he began.

It was John's wife.

"Where the fuck have you been?" Margret shrieked into the phone.

"I'm here at the office attending to business," he told her.

"Monkey business," Margret quipped. "You were supposed to come home after that concert tonight. Of course, it was a sellout, and you're probably high on something."

"Nothing stronger than grass, love," he told her.

"You'd better not get in anything stronger," Margret reminded him. "You know the conditions of your probation, dear."

Trying to calm her down, he explained that he was only working hard all night at the office so that he could buy beautiful things for her.

"You've got a good gift of gab, John," she told him, "but I don't believe a word of it. I've heard your lies too many times."

She hung up the phone angrily. John paced the floor. Margret was becoming a real problem. She had been his secretary before he hired Susan Moore. Susan had told him that she thought a private investigator was tailing her. This made John nervous. He didn't want to go through the costly divorce court proceedings. More than that, he'd had a child by Margret, and it bothered him to think of leaving his young son with her.

Finally, he returned to the office party. At this point, he realized he had promised to switch from cock sucking to cunt lapping.

"All right," John called out, trying to forget what his wife had told him, "let's switch from cock sucking to pussy eating."

The girls were glad for a breather. It had been a difficult run carrying on like this. Swinging over now, Susan stretched out her legs.

"See what a good tongue you've got, John," she told him.

John was anxious to suck on her cunt. If there was one thing he enjoyed, it was eating pussy.

"Come on, baby," she told him with a glint in her eyes that told him how much she wanted him to go down on her.

John urgently began licking at her cunt. He let out a lustful groan as his mouth smacked into her swollen pussy, muffling the sound moistly.

Susan began writhing underneath him as she felt him licking hungrily down there. He let his tongue lick at her damp flesh, wiggling her clitoris and opening her sizzling cleft ever wider. His tongue poked aggressively at her heated slit. As Susan felt John's tongue licking up and down her cunt she cried out in passionate abandon.

"Lick it. Get your tongue in me. Yes. I love that!"

John was plunging deep into her vagina with his tongue now, fucking her for all it was worth, sloshing his saliva up and down her slit. Her clitoris tingled to his every touch. The encircling muscles of her cunt mouth grasped at his slippery tongue. John kept his hands on Susan's firm, round ass cheeks as she ground her pelvis in his face. She kept bucking back at him. It was obvious how much she wanted it.

"Suck me, suck me," Susan begged.

The record promoter's hot tongue plunged into her vagina like a penis. When he pulled his tongue out of her clutching, slippery hole, he swabbed up and down heatedly along the length of her soft split, stroking her firm, throbbing clit with its velvety hood, her splayed lips, which oozed juice, providing his tongue with a tantalizing taste of her.

Then he licked even further. He was attracted by the curvaceous swells of her buttocks as he spread her thighs wider apart, forcing her to expose her entire nakedness to his gaze. Panting now, she felt him licking her there. The tickling sensation of his tongue lashing at the sensitive, inner slopes of her satiny buttocks had her completely excited now.

"I'm going to swing around," he told her as he quit licking her ass cheeks, "so you can suck my prick and lick my butt, too."

At this point, she was eager to express what she felt for John. He had provided her with such a wonderful job as well as erotic thrills that she could hardly wait to lick and suck on his sexual organs. John swung his body around so his crotch was even with her face. And then he returned his attention to her cunt. Patricia caught what was happening out of the corner of her eye. She objected.

"That's not fair," she called out. "This is pussy-eating time."

John laughed as he swung around and went back to licking

at her pussy. It was obvious that was what he was supposed to do. He licked up and down with long, lusty thrusts, hungrily tasting her juicy vagina. In the meantime, he glanced up to watch what was happening on the television.

Ziggy Falcon was talking to Jennifer Davis, trying to convince her that she ought to let him sodomize her.

"A lot of people like it better from behind," he told her. "Let's try it that way."

Even though she thought it was a disgusting act, t she wanted it. Anything to please Ziggy, as she had fallen for him like a ton of bricks.

"If you say so, Ziggy," Jennifer said in her little girl voice.

Susan Moore was so angry now she could only think of one thing. She wanted to aim her pearl-handled pistol at Ziggy Falcon and end this debacle. It was disgusting that her lovely girlfriend should be subjected to such perverse sex as this.

"Now, baby," he told her, "let me get some lubrication for your asshole."

The office orgy erupted in laughter as they watched what was happening next on the closed-circuit television screen coming from the penthouse suite atop the high-rise building.

Jennifer Davis was forced to kneel on the floor.

"Right here in front of this mirror," Ziggy guided her over to a corner.

Once she was in a kneeling position, he got down behind her and used some lubrication on her asshole.

"I always keep some lube handy," he told her, "because I never know when I'm gonna meet a girl and want to sodomize her."

"I guess you've done this before," Jennifer told him.

"You bet your cute ass I have," the rock star assured the college graduate.

Ziggy parted Jennifer's satiny ass cheeks. His penis was slippery, and he had applied some of the slick substance to her anal opening. When she was bent over far enough, he figured he could guide his massive manhood up her ass crack. At this angle, he shoved forward suddenly.

"Fuck your asshole," he told her as he rammed it to her.

"Ohhh," she gasped, "I can't stand it."

He was cramming his cock right up her behind.

"You're hurting me," she objected.

Jennifer's response to the anal assault of the rock star's throbbing manhood brought varied reactions from the office-orgy watchers. The women thought it was disgusting and perverse. However, the men seemed to obtain a certain kind of warped, sadistic glee from observing it happening.

"That's awful," Susan Moore erupted as she saw her female lover being assaulted from behind.

"Awful nice," John Williams smirked. "I'll bet she's real tight. I wish that I was in Ziggy's position."

The rock star closed his eyes as he let his huge cock tip slip past her tight anal opening. He shook his head from side to side, obviously savoring the delicious excitement that he was experiencing as he rammed his prick up her rectum.

"Up your asshole," he gasped as he rutted up her butt. "Oh, baby, you're beautiful. Fuck it, fuck it."

With determination and drive, he shamelessly worked his

prick up her tight anal passage. Jennifer swung her hips as he invaded her tight opening ever deeper.

"Ohhh, I can't stand it," she groaned as she felt him riding up her rectum.

Ziggy Falcon tugged at Jennifer's legs and parted them until he had plenty of room to maneuver. Now he had a direct shot at her hot ass.

"Relax," he told her as he rammed in deeper.

Jennifer was holding her breath now, closing her eyes, barely able to stand it. His initial instinct was to shove forward with everything he had. He knew that such an approach would result in a speedy orgasm. Even though he felt like working his cock rapidly, he seesawed his prick back and forth slowly and steadily. Even that type of approach appeared to be too much for Jennifer, who let out several gasps.

"Shut up, Jennifer," he warned her, "and let me screw you."

The London rock star drilled the girl's ass several times. He was letting the tempo of his cock in her ass build up until he really rammed it into her.

"You make such beautiful music," he told her. "Just shove back to me."

Ziggy's penis was rigid, long, and stimulated by her very presence. Tiny waves of tingly delight bolted through his hard rod as he continued driving it in and out of her, letting the pace build, permitting the sweltering excitement inside him to wildly generate. The longer he kept up his movements, the hotter he became. As the intensity of the screwing pace accelerated, he felt more of a blinding need to thrill her with hard, deep, piercing strokes.

"Sodomy is the only way to fuck," he gasped as he rode up her tight anus.

The more intently and deeply that Ziggy drove, the more painful the looks that surfaced on Jennifer's face. She let out several anguished gasps after one hot series of forward strokes. Ziggy retaliated by reaching out and slapping her.

"That's just a tiny dose of what you'd get if you don't shut up," he warned her. "Most women love me. They beg me to screw 'em. Now, don't try to wreck my ego by saying you don't enjoy my sodomizing you."

This bothered her. She let out a few occasional gasps, but they were soft and almost noiseless, so he couldn't complain. All the while, Ziggy continued stabbing closer toward orgasm. It felt good to apply his penis with vigorous skill. And it felt even better to derive sensation from her tight, beautiful asshole.

"You're a virgin ass, too, baby," he told her. "I can tell. I sure hit the jackpot tonight."

At this point, it was hurting her so badly that she could barely hold back her anguished cries. His slick, hard prick was ramming all the way up her asshole. Ziggy's lust-bloated balls slapping lewdly on her upturned buttocks excited him all the more.

"If you're gonna suffer, damn it," he exclaimed, "you'd better do it in silence."

Then Ziggy gripped her buttock cheek, pinching tightly as his huge prick continued stabbing rhythmically in and out of her. He lifted his body forward with eagerness, driving his hot prick into her with all of his might. Tears began to splash down Jennifer's cheeks as she realized he was not going to stop until he got his rocks off. Ziggy intensified his cock stabs, which became sharper and even deeper. In the meantime, this was providing plenty of erotic excitement for the men who were going down on the office women.

John Williams was sucking hungrily on Susan Moore's pussy, and she figured she'd give him a jolt. She didn't want to give him her juices. She was so angry at him now that she decided to take charge of the office sex orgy. The pussy-sucking circle was going to be switched to another person now.

"Change pussies," she cried out excitedly. "Go ahead, do it."

Patricia, who was nearby, was disappointed. She was about to juice in her lover's face and openly complained.

"Just when I was there," Patricia panted.

It made no difference. The cock-sucking circle had switched when John called "Change," and now everybody was listening to Susan. Suddenly, Susan sensed a surge of power and authority. She knew very well that John was married. She also knew that Margret, his wife, was someone he feared and dreaded. If John wouldn't give Jennifer back to her so she could take her away forever from this horrible rock star, she reasoned she might appear as a witness in a divorce trial on Margret's side.

That would be enough to get John right where she wanted him. John looked at her with disgust as he moved to the next girl in line. However, the naked young blonde who was throwing her legs over John's shoulders was pleased. She felt perhaps if the boss ate her cunt he might get the hots for her all the time and it would help her with her job at the office.

"Hey, tiger, let's see how good your tongue is," she smiled up at him.

John enjoyed licking the girl that he was making it with now. His hot hands reached up to grip her lush breasts. Then he massaged her moistening vagina. The young office girl liked the way he touched the downy, soft, curly pubic hair. As John let his fingers smoothly slide between the moist pink lips of her pussy, he could feel her jutting red clit, quivering and hard.

It became so intensely exciting as he rubbed his fingers over her clit that she was conscious of her juices now. Becoming more aroused, she parted her legs and thrust her pelvis forward. John got his hot mouth down there and began licking. The loud slurping sounds of his mouth pressed tightly against her hot cunt as she ground into his face excited her.

"Lick it, tiger," she panted as his tongue drove wildly into her deep, feminine crevice.

Reaching out, he gripped her lush, jiggling bosoms. The girl's nipples were taut as she thrust her hips forward.

While Susan was being sucked by the next man in line, she was oblivious to his tongue stabs in her fiery, hot cunt. She was thinking and plotting. She was reasoning how easy it would be to put John in his place and pay him for what was happening at this terrible orgy that she was forced to endure. The office orgy had turned into a debacle. There was Jennifer, her reputation ruined, as Ziggy Falcon pumped his manhood up her tight anus.

It was awful having to endure this. Somehow, Susan felt

guilty. If it hadn't been for the fact that she had brought her out here, this never would have happened. The excitement of working at a rock record company diminished instantly. Noticing that she wasn't putting her all into her lovemaking, her male lover complained.

"Bring your cunt in my face, honey," he told her. "Put some passion into your pussy."

Looking at him, Susan suddenly forced a smile on her face.

"I'm sorry," she whispered.

Her young, husky, hairy lover was gazing down hotly at her ripe, full, naked bosoms. He pinched the nipples as he once more brought his face over her cunt. His tongue licked her juicy crevice, and then he suddenly gripped her buttocks and pulled her tighter to him. Soon, he was stabbing inside of her moist crotch. Devastating thrills went through him as his tongue swept over her pussy.

"Ohhh, yes," she panted as he licked her quivering, pink flesh.

The fragrant aroma of her enticing cuntal opening propelled his tongue into action. The young hairy, husky office man slid his tongue slowly up and down the length of her welcoming vaginal folds. At this point, Susan was moaning aloud, unable to struggle against him any longer. His fiery, hot tongue was pumping into her pussy in a depraved, obscene way.

Anxiously his hot hands gripped the soft globes of her buttocks as he buried his face in her crotch, tongue fucking her in pistoning movements. He was probing deeper, ever deeper inside her throbbing, aroused vagina. Tears streaked down her cheeks as she trembled with wanton lust. The muscular young man was feasting on her pussy, his tongue lapping, licking, sucking noisily as he fired her up.

"Ohhh, ahhh, yes, eat me!"

Unable to struggle against her own carnal cravings any longer, she was whimpering with desire as her lover's tongue kept flicking in and out of the pouting lips of her pussy. Lustfully he sucked on her erect clitoris. His teeth bore down gently as he nibbled her there. All of her defenses vanished. It was happening as she gazed down at his head between her legs through lust-blurred eyes.

"Suck me, suck me," she whispered.

His hot tongue was lashing lewdly at her exposed pussy, and then he got his face right in there and sucked until she gushed. The sexual ecstasy that surged through her body now as she was coming in his mouth had her gasping into an animalistic frenzy.

"Ohhh, ahhh, I'm coming – ahhhhh!"

The warmly seeping walls of her cunt were being voraciously licked by her lover's lewd tongue. Hungrily, his long digit lapped her up, making the sensitive area of her clitoris tingle with delight, momentarily blotting out the performance that was taking place on the screen.

Some of the others in the office orgy, however, were looking up at Ziggy Falcon driving his prick in Jennifer Davis' asshole with such deep penetrating jabs they figured he might tear her apart. Ziggy was really turned on.

"Ohhh, I never had an ass fuck like this," he explained passionately. "Fuck me, fuck me."

John's eyes feasted on what was taking place on the

television screen. How he wished he could trade places with Ziggy Falcon. That would allow him to try out a delicious new girl. But this was Ziggy Falcon's moment, and he was making the most of it.

"Fuck, fuck," Ziggy panted as he pumped it up her tight asshole. "Swing your butt, baby."

Reaching underneath her, he fingered her cunt. He gripped the nub of her clitoris and squeezed it as he drove in all the way and exploded.

"Ohhh, I'm coming," he gasped as he unloaded his throbbing penis in her asshole.

Her buttocks twisted in an erotic frenzy as his coming provided lubrication for his slick, long shaft. His fingers pulled from her pussy, and his hands caressed her satiny bare buttocks as he savored the delicious sensation of unloading his juice in her asshole.

Having finished sodomizing her, he withdrew. Then he pressed against her ass cheeks, and some more sperm spurted out of his penis tip. He had given such a performance that some of the office girls applauded.

Looking up at the television screen, John Williams couldn't help but comment to the man who was nearby.

"Yes, I believe I'd better hire her," he said.

Everyone at the office orgy erupted in wild gales of laughter. That is, except for Susan Moore. Susan was seething with resentment and rage at the perverse spectacle. Her eyes caught sight of the series of naked pictures of women that lined the walls. John had joked about being a sex maniac the first time she applied for a job, and his eyes had focused on her legs. The pictures of the naked women in various suggestive positions should have been enough to inform her of what she was getting into. However, she was so anxious to obtain employment at that moment she hadn't considered it. Now, she had to consider a lot of things. And the day's first order was to get Jennifer Davis out of the clutches of the rock idol. She didn't want that to go on any longer.

THE END

A Story from

Yesteryear's Stories Reflected Today
Yabot AB
www.yabot.se